Donald Duck Sees South America

WALT DISNEY STORY BOOKS

DONALD DUCK SEES
SOUTH AMERICA

Told by

H. MARION PALMER

Illustrated by

THE WALT DISNEY STUDIO

D. C. HEATH AND COMPANY
BOSTON

D. C. HEATH AND COMPANY

NEW YORK   BOSTON   CHICAGO

ATLANTA   SAN FRANCISCO   DALLAS   LONDON

Contents

CHAPTER I

Donald Sets Out

"Are you going to just one country or all the way round South America?" asked the travel agent.

"All the way round, of course," said Donald, tracing a big circle in the air over the ticket counter. "I've seen my own country. Now it's time for me to see other countries in my hemisphere."

"Quite right, sir," said the man, pulling out an enormous string of orange tickets. "Are you going by plane or by boat?"

"I'm a person of action," said Donald, impatiently. "I fly, of course."

"Hmmmmm," said the man, looking Donald up and down very critically. "How's your priority?"

"My what?"

"I mean are you an ambassador, a rear admiral, a major general, a director of Latin-American affairs? To get to South America by plane these days, you have to be important enough to get a priority. They may put you off the plane if you're not important."

"Oh, there's no worry about that," laughed Donald.

"You just give me the tickets." Donald reached for his wallet and pulled out a thick roll of bills. "By the way, what sort of clothes do I take?"

"Only necessities—but remember that south of the equator the seasons are reversed. Take winter clothes for the summer, and summer clothes for the winter; thick clothes for the south, where it's cold; thin clothes for the north, where it's hot. Put in your sail-fishing clothes and your condor-hunting clothes. You most certainly will need your mummy-digging clothes in Chan Chan, Peru—"

"But—" said Donald.

"Don't interrupt me. Take mosquito netting for camping in the jungle marshes of the Amazon. You'll need your riding clothes, spurs, and your polo clothes for week ends on the big ranches in the Argentine. You'll need bite-proof puttees to protect your ankles at the snake farm in São Paulo, Brazil—"

"Snake farm!" gulped Donald.

"Don't interrupt me," the travel agent hurried on. "Be sure to take your white dinner jacket for dancing at the Rio Casino, bathing clothes for the beach at the Copacabaña, and a costume for the Carnival. For August in the Chilean lakes you must have skis, ski boots, ski wax, a couple of splints, and your first-aid kit. By all means take a bottle of sodium bicarbonate, because if you'll pardon me, sir, you appear to be the type of person who will eat altogether too much rare beefsteak in Buenos Aires."

"O.K. Have them pick up my trunks tomorrow."

"Trunks!" gasped the man, looking down at Donald with horrified disdain. "When you travel by air, you'll have to carry everything in a handbag."

Donald grabbed his tickets and walked away. Everything in a handbag! What a situation!

"Just one more thing," called the man. "Have you any diseases? Have you ever been arrested?"

"Most certainly not!" answered Donald angrily.

"Most fortunate. You must bring a certificate of vaccination from your doctor, your finger prints, and a certificate of good character from the police. South Americans are nice people, and they are very particular whom they let into their countries."

It seemed almost impossible for Donald to get everything done and get to the airport at four on Friday. But he did.

Passengers were already going up the gangway of the sleek, shimmering airliner when Donald arrived. The purser in a smart blue uniform bowed to him and ushered him up on board. His seat was by a window. He sank down on the spongy cushions, relaxed, and gazed around. Everybody looked important. A Navy officer was already in a seat behind him, having an orangeade.

Donald was so excited that his mouth felt like cotton. He ordered an orangeade, too.

The pilot was racing the two mighty motors. Outside, the ground crew was standing by to pull out the blocks from under the wheels. The visitors were taking out their handkerchiefs to wave good-by.

The purser was coming up the aisle toward Donald. He stopped beside the chair and bowed. "I'm sorry, sir, but we've just had orders from Washington. Your seat to South America will be occupied by *El Presidente de la Comisión de la América Latina.*"

"Who?" demanded Donald.

5

"*El Presi*—never mind! I haven't time to repeat it. It's time to take off. Come along, get ready."

"You mean I'm not to go?" gasped Donald.

"No, not with us," said the purser with dreadful politeness, hustling Donald on with his coat, "but there are other ways to go."

The purser took down Donald's bag from the luggage rack and handed him his hat. Donald had to get up. Everyone was looking at him.

He was so mad that he could hardly walk, but he followed the purser down the aisle to the door.

"Oh, sir!" called out a rippling feminine voice behind him. Donald wheeled about. It was the stewardess. "Your orangeade, sir," she said. "You may take it with you and drink it on the ground."

As Donald plodded down the gangway, sadly clutching his bottle and two straws, a tall man in striped pants and a high silk hat bustled past him, going up!

Donald turned his back and strode off the field. He did not care to wave to *El Presidente de la Comisión de la América Latina*.

The next day Donald took the boat.

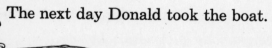

6

CHAPTER II

All about South America

"Hmmm — hmmm!" said someone with a deep voice, clearing his throat. "They tell me you are going to South America for the first time."

"Yes, first time," mumbled Donald, without looking up. He had just tucked himself under a blanket in his deck chair. He had his diary and a pencil. He had been on board five days and had not written a thing. Now he was going to begin.

"So you are a 'first-timer,'" said the voice. It came from the next deck chair, hardly one foot away from Donald's left ear. "I've been around South America for thirty years. My name's Whelpley. What I don't know about South America isn't worth knowing. Just exactly where are you going on your trip?"

"Everywhere," sighed Donald, digging in deeper under the blanket and trying to concentrate on his diary. "I don't want to miss a thing."

"You don't want to miss a thing!" The voice laughed out loud. "Then you'll have to cover seven million square miles!"

"That's just what I'd like to do," said Donald. "I want to see it all. I want to meet foreign people, too, Spanish people and Indians, all the different tribes of Indians."

The voice laughed scoffingly. "I see you don't know much about South America. If you want to talk to all the Indians, you'll have to be a lot smarter than most people are with languages. In addition to Spanish, I suppose you talk Pano, Chibcha, Araucan, Chocho, Arawak. No doubt you'll be able to order your breakfast at Macchu Picchu in perfect Inca."

"I'll manage to order it," said Donald, "and to pay for it, too."

8

The voice chuckled again. "Then I suppose you understand all about foreign moneys! Can you make change quickly in any sort of money — sucres, libras, pesos, cruzeires, or bolivars? Do you know just how many betel nuts to trade for a pair of sheepskin boots and a sombrero?"

"I'm very good at bargaining. If anyone cheats me, I'll call a lawyer."

"Can you do it in Spanish?" the voice went on. "I'll bet you don't even know the names of the countries we are coming to, or what they produce. Come now, do you?"

"I'm busy," said Donald. "I want to write in my diary."

"Do you know where that warm wool blanket you're all wrapped up in came from? It came from Peru." The blanket was rudely pulled back. "Wake up and look at yourself! Look at what you're wearing! Why, if it weren't for South America, you'd be practically naked!"

Donald sat up quickly and looked himself over. Then he looked at Mr. Whelpley, who was middle-aged and fattish, and had deep sunburned furrows on his face. In his lap was a half-empty box of enormous green gumdrops.

"That beautiful, soft sport jacket," Mr. Whelpley went on, running his fingers down Donald's lapels, "is made of vicuña wool. It comes from little vicuñas that live only on the highest plateaus in Peru. And look at the lining. That's made of alpaca. It comes from Peru, too.

"Look at your wrist watch!" said Mr. Whelpley, grabbing Donald's arm. "Before someone in the United States could make that watch for you, someone like me had to find the gold for it in the gravel of some South American river. And those buttons on your coat!" He pulled one right off.

"Hey!" said Donald. "Go easy!"

"That button," said Mr. Whelpley, holding it up
under Donald's nose for him to examine, "was once
an ivory nut, growing on a tree in Ecuador."

"Anyway," said Donald, "my sneakers did not come
from South America!"

"Certainly they did. It probably took a tree along
the Amazon about five years to grow the latex for
those rubber soles. Now lean back a minute. Open
your mouth and say *Ah!*"

Donald didn't want to open his mouth and say

Ah! for this pest. He started to get up, but Mr. Whelpley jerked him backwards, yanked down his lower jaw, and peered in. "Hmmmm. I see a silver filling there in your third molar. Some miner down in Colombia probably dug that up for you."

With a terrific heave, Donald finally broke away from Mr. Whelpley, and raced off down the deck. What a conceited know-it-all that man was! He'd find that Donald would get even with him! Donald went inside to the library steward.

"Give me every book you have on South America," said Donald. "I want to find out where every country is, how-do-you-spell-it, and what they've got there."

"Tonight?" gasped the library steward.

"Tonight. I haven't a moment to lose."

It took the library steward, the assistant library steward, and all the smoking room stewards to carry down the books from thirty shelves to Donald's cabin. Then Caspar, Donald's room steward, brought a globe, an atlas, a whole plate of corned beef sandwiches, and an extra reading lamp.

Caspar stayed for a few minutes after the others had gone. He was examining the titles of the books: "*Coffee Bean Culture*, volumes I, II, and III; *How to*

Make Poison Arrows, by a Head-hunter of the Amazon; *Long Division as Practiced by the Early Incas*." Caspar shook his head in bewilderment. "Well, good night, sir. I guess you'll be studying very late."

"Yes, very late," said Donald.

"Brain work like yours must be very exhausting. Good night, sir." Caspar closed the door and disappeared.

It was extremely warm in the cabin. Donald opened the porthole. A soft tropical wind blew through his hair. Way, way off on the sea outside, he could see the twinkling lights of other ships. Donald's ship was approaching Cristobal, the port on the Atlantic side of the Panama Canal.

Donald put on his pajamas, climbed into his bunk with the plate of sandwiches, and leaned out the open porthole. More and more lights danced on the horizon; they came nearer; here and there he could see the white foamy paths of ships passing by. Strange, delicious smells filled the air—coffee, cocoa, bananas, caraway seeds. There were dozens and dozens of strange-smelling smells he had never smelled before.

Donald felt less and less like studying. In a few minutes he fell asleep.

13

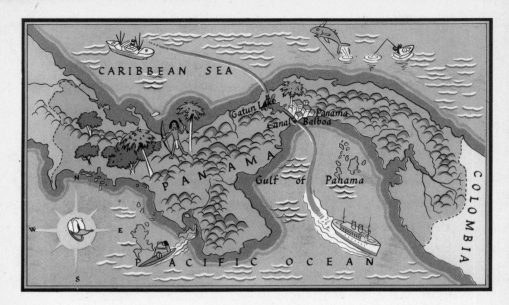

CHAPTER III

Through the Panama Canal

Clank! Spttt! Oink! Bells were ringing, whistles tooting. Iron chains clanged through hawse-holes.

Donald woke up with a terrible start, knocking over his reading lamp and the whole seven volumes of *The History of Peru*. He grabbed at his wrist watch. "Quarter to six! We must be starting through the Canal!" He climbed into his clothes and rushed pell-mell up to the promenade deck.

No one was in sight. Not a single other passenger was up and around yet, but, to Donald's great

14

delight, the deck was all covered with tables spread with bright yellow tablecloths. Breakfast was going to be served outdoors, so that the passengers could see the Canal as they ate.

Donald sat down at a table by the rail. The ship was nosing into a narrow passage between two concrete platforms. There were railroad tracks and an electric locomotive on each platform, and a dozen or more bare-chested men in enormous straw hats. A whistle blew! Steel cables were flung out from both sides of the ship. The men grabbed them and quickly fastened them to the rear ends of the locomotives. A bell rang! With a hum the engines started forward on their tracks. They were pulling the boat into a concrete chamber. A man in a high watchtower ahead pulled a lever. Mammoth steel gates came out from the sides of the platforms and closed behind the boat. It was in a lock!

Suddenly the water below began to churn up. It boiled! It was rising! The ship was being raised up—up to the water level of a higher lock beyond.

When the lock was filled, like a giant bathtub, the gates in front swung open, and again the engines pulled the ship forward.

"Whew!" exclaimed Donald. "What an elevator!"

15

"How about some breakfast?" asked someone, sitting down in the chair beside him. It was the Captain. He was smiling and pleasant in a crisp white uniform with plenty of gold braid. "What shall we have first? I'm hungry."

"I always have orange juice," stammered Donald. Never before in his life had he sat at the table with a captain. If only that *Presidente* person who had taken his seat in the plane could see him now!

The Captain clapped his hands for the Chief Steward, who came with a pad and pencil and stood at attention, waiting for orders. "We'll start with tropical fruits," ordered the Captain. "Bring some papayas, not too soft, white pineapple, pomegranates, and chirimoyas."

The Chief Steward clicked his heels and disappeared.

"Well," said the Captain after a few minutes, "what do you think of the Canal?" They were going through another lock, just like the first one.

"It seems like a simple job," answered Donald. "Just digging a ditch. Anybody could do that."

The Captain laughed. "The Panama Canal isn't merely a ditch. It's actually a stairway that goes up over some mountains and down the other side."

16

Donald felt delightfully important as the stewards came with whole trayfuls of breakfast.

The ship had climbed through three locks now, and was moving gently on under its own power toward a big, sprawling lake in the middle of a jungle. Over to the right was a mammoth dam, where endless gallons of water were shooting down over a broad spillway. There were power houses around it and United States Army buildings, with soldiers drilling in front.

"We're crossing Gatun Lake," the Captain continued, finishing his last mouthful of pancake. "It's the largest artificial lake in the world—and. it sits right on top of what used to be a forest. If you look out beyond those channel markers, you can see the tops of the old trees, sticking up through the water. Come with me." The Captain threw his napkin down. "You can see it better from the bridge."

Nobody could go on the bridge unless he was specially invited. "I've made an impression," thought Donald. "It did not take him long to pick me out."

The first officer on watch saluted as they stepped off the ladder onto the bridge. The Captain handed a pair of binoculars to Donald.

Through the powerful magnifying lenses, the whole

lake seemed suddenly to be alive. "Look! Look!" shouted Donald. The specks on the distant half-submerged tree stumps became yellow parrots and long-necked white egrets. Donald scanned the dense jungle of the shore line. "Where are the mountains? I don't see a single one."

"We're cruising directly over them," said the Captain, pointing down.

The lake grew narrower; the shore rose steeply.

"This is the Gaillard Cut," continued the Cap-

tain. "For about eight miles, it slices right through the spine of the American continent. Look at those hills and think of the digging that had to be done! Think of the job it was just to prop up those hills and keep them from landsliding down!"

"When do we get to the Pacific?" Donald asked.

"As soon as we go through the Pacific Locks at the end of this Cut. Now that the ship has come safely upstairs and across the mountains, it has to go downstairs to get to the level of the Pacific. The locks work just the way they did on the Atlantic side, except that they will let us down instead of up. Now, my friend, I'm afraid I'll have to ask you to excuse me. I must get dressed for an important engagement."

Donald thanked the Captain most politely for the good time they had had together. Then he ran down the bridge ladder to the deck. He was bursting with importance. The Captain had singled him out, him, of all the passengers on the boat, for a visit to the bridge.

At the bottom of the ladder, Donald bumped straight into Mr. Whelpley, waiting for someone.

"How do you do?" said Donald loftily. "The Captain and I have been chatting up on the bridge."

19

"I do hope you learned something," sighed Mr. Whelpley. "Going through the Canal, the Skipper always tries to explain it to some ignoramus."

"Ignoramus! Why, you—you—" Donald sputtered.

The Captain appeared at the top of the ladder in his tennis clothes. "Sorry to keep you waiting, Whelpley," he said as he came down, "but I had to finish a little educational job."

"A hopeless job," laughed Mr. Whelpley.

"Oh, not too hopeless," answered the Captain. "He'll learn something—before the cruise is over." He smiled at Donald as he strode off with Mr. Whelpley toward the tennis court.

CHAPTER IV

Three Cities of Panama

When the ship reached the big docks at the Pacific end of the Canal, Donald was the first passenger off the gangplank.

"Take me to the town," he ordered, climbing into a taxicab.

The driver was dozing placidly under an immense straw hat. He was right in the middle of his afternoon siesta. He yawned at Donald. "Which town?"

"*The* town, of course. Wake up!"

21

The driver yawned again and stretched. "We have three towns."

"Great heavens! Three towns! Then for goodness' sake, wake up! I've got to see them all."

They sped away from the hustle and commotion of the dock and the throngs of excited passengers perspiring in the tropic heat. In a few minutes they were driving down a broad avenue lined with beautiful vine-covered bungalows, brilliant gardens of oleander, bougainvillea, and bright yellow jasmine.

"Which town is this?" asked Donald. "I like it."

"Balboa—United States town. People here work for Canal." The driver spoke with a foreign accent, using only a few words. The rest he said with his eyebrows, his shoulders, and his hands. He pointed to the hill ahead. "Hospital."

So this was the hospital the Americans had built. Donald had heard that its doctors were famous all over the world. They knew about all the germs and fevers that attack people who live in hot climates; they had invented medicines, serums, and pills to cure the sick, not only here, but even in China, Africa, and Thailand.

Donald leaned forward and tapped the driver. "You know, I'm an American and proud of it."

"Me too. Much proud to be American."

Donald was puzzled. "If you're American, why do you speak the American language with a foreign accent?"

The driver was getting excited. "I not speak my American language with foreign accent. I only speak your American language with foreign accent. You, North American. Me, Latin American."

Donald thought for a few minutes. Then he leaped into the front seat. "Now I see! We're both Americans! It's only the language that's different. We're friends! Shake, pal. What's your name?"

"Alfredo."

"Alfredo, I'm Donald."

Donald shook Alfredo's hand. Then Alfredo shook Donald's hand. Then they laughed. Then they shook hands again. Then Alfredo flung his arms around Donald. He patted and slapped him on the shoulders. "*Mi amigo, mi amigo Donaldo. Alfredo y Donaldo, amigos*—friends." He kept saying it over and over again as they drove along.

They passed the Casino, the bullfighting ring, the race track, and a whole long freight train filled with green bananas, coming from the plantations to be shipped away. Then they came to

an old stone bridge over a dusty dried-up moat.

"What's this? Looks as if it once was something."

"Bridge to old city, old Panama. But look! All gone!" Alfredo bumped to a stop.

Beyond the bridge Donald could see crumbling ruins of buildings, a piece of the wall of a tower, stones jutting up through masses of snarled vine. "Whew! What happened?" he asked.

Alfredo shrugged his shoulders hopelessly and sighed. "Pirates!"

"Pirates? What pirates? Spanish pirates?"

"No! No! British pirates! Henry Morgan's pirates. Big swords!" Alfredo strode up to the edge of the bridge and began brandishing an imaginary sword.

"They rush across bridge, cut Spaniards down. Splash! Then Morgan men—they rush upon city."

"What then, Alfredo? Was there a big fight?"

"Much, much fight! Everyone get killed! Pirates grab everything, all silver, all gold." Alfredo's eyes shone widely at the thought of so much treasure.

Donald was poking around through the brambles and briars, hoping to find something that the pirates had forgotten; but he found only stones, and lizards and spiders. "The pirates got everything," he said sadly. "There's nothing left of old Panama!"

"But now, Donaldo, I show you new Panama!" Alfredo led Donald off from the ruins. "Spaniards very smart people. Right away quick they build new city, bigger walls, more beautiful."

Together they rattled on into new Panama. The narrow, steep, cobbled streets and balconied windows looked just like pictures Donald had seen of old Spain. The houses had bright flowerpots at every window; sometimes, through a doorway, he could look into a square courtyard or patio, with fountains and tall, shading trees. "Tonight," he thought to himself, "I'll write about this in my diary. Tonight is the night to begin."

They turned into a broad plaza. A band was playing, and the people of Panama were promenading around and around. Donald said good-by to Alfredo and joined the sauntering parade.

Soon he decided it was time for a snack. He went into a café, and sat down at a little table. The place was already rather crowded with noisy passengers from the ship.

"I'd like a ham sandwich," said Donald to the waiter.

Someone at the next table laughed. Donald turned around. It was Mr. Whelpley. In front of him was a big bowl of little red fishy things. They looked like midget lobsters. He was picking them up by the tail, dipping them into some sauce, and swallowing them, eyes, tails, claws, and everything.

"Crayfish from Chile," said Mr. Whelpley, smacking his lips. "Delicious! And you order a ham sandwich! Why, you don't know the first thing about how to order in Panama!"

Donald glowered. He snatched up the menu and beckoned for the waiter to come back.

"Bring me," ordered Donald in a voice loud enough so Mr. Whelpley could not miss it, "some mussels on the half shell, some boiled snails, fried octopus, and a crab soufflé. Then I'll have a Mexican tortilla with wild rice and bumalo fish. Bring me also a flank of Argentine beef with bamboo shoots and red peppers. For dessert, I'll have preserved figs, chirimoyas, litchi nuts, and Chinese ginger."

Donald chuckled. He could hear Mr. Whelpley gasp. This time he had shown that man something!

Donald tried bravely to eat the whole order. But something inside of him went wrong. In the midst of the wild rice and bumalo fish, he collapsed.

Mr. Whelpley and the waiter carried his limp body through the streets of Panama, back to the ship. Somehow, when Donald woke up later that night in his cabin, he did not feel much like writing in his diary. He did not even care that the next time he went ashore he would be in South America.

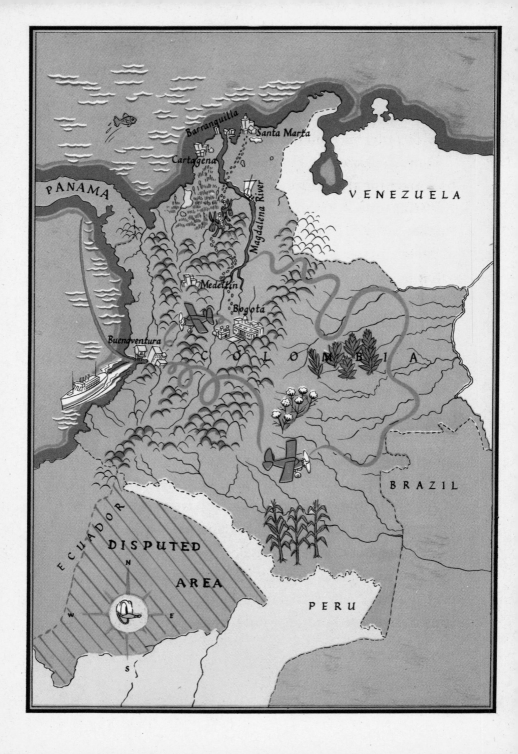

CHAPTER V

Donald Covers Colombia

"We're coming to Buenaventura," shouted Donald. "I want to go ashore." He banged again on the window of the purser's office, which was pulled down tight.

"I want to go ashore at Buenaventura," repeated Donald loudly. "I need some Colombian money!"

The window snapped up abruptly. The white-uniformed purser wrinkled his forehead. "How much?"

"How much do I need?"

"For what?"

"To see the country. That's what I'm here for."

"To see the whole country?" The purser seemed surprised.

"Certainly the whole country! Every bit of the country. I don't want to miss a thing."

The purser raised his eyebrows. "You should have informed us before, sir, that you were here to inspect the whole country. We shall be most happy to advise you. Won't you come inside?" He opened the side door of the office and Donald went in.

The purser folded his arms and began walking up and down. "Now let's see. You've got more than four hundred thousand square miles to cover—"

"O.K.," interrupted Donald. "Where do I begin?"

"With the big plantations," said the assistant purser, "where you'll see how they grow sugar, cocoa, coffee, and bananas by the millions—"

"Are you interested in precious metals and jewels?" questioned the purser, walking faster and thinking harder. "You'll have to visit the mines."

"You mustn't omit a little side trip through the jungles," added the assistant purser excitedly, "to hunt crocodiles, pythons, jaguars, and sloths."

"Wonderful!" exclaimed Donald. "How long will it take?"

The purser thought for a minute. "A trip of this sort will take you just about six months."

"Wow!" cried Donald. He whizzed past the pursers and shot through the door. Six months! He had only a few days to do the whole job.

Down the gangway and out through the pier he went in a flash. Donald raced up the little winding main street of Buenaventura.

The houses looked peculiar; they perched high off the ground on tall stilts. Some roofs were of straw, while others were made of metal, corrugated like the cardboard around a package. On the side streets swampy water sloshed up under the houses, and small boats and canoes were tied right to the steps.

"*Oiga!*" someone called out to Donald. It was a Negro in a red shirt and yellow hat, lounging in a canoe underneath his own front porch. "*Oiga!*" He beckoned. He had something in a straw basket.

"What is it?" In the bottom of the basket was a fuzzy brown ball of fur, breathing softly.

"You buy?" The Negro looked at Donald hopefully.

"Buy? What is it?" Donald shook the basket. "Hey! What are you? Wake up!"

The fur ball quietly just went on breathing. Donald poked it.

"You'll never wake him up that way," said the familiar voice of Mr. Whelpley right over Donald's shoulder. "It's a kinkajou, sometimes called a honey bear. What I don't know about those things isn't worth knowing. They're nocturnal—"

"They're what?" said Donald.

"Nocturnal. That's a two-dollar word for saying they like to sleep all day and run around all night. Here, I'll show you how to wake him up."

Mr. Whelpley took a pink carnation out of his buttonhole. He stuck it in Donald's buttonhole, picked up the drowsy animal, and put him on Donald's shoulder. Suddenly the honey bear breathed harder. A little sharp-nosed face appeared and a long red tongue shot out, so long that it almost seemed to come from way back in his tail. It darted into the flower, pulled out some petals, and sucked out the juice from their ends.

"Well, I'll be jiggered!" said Donald, as the creature started tearing the carnation to shreds. "Will I buy him!" He handed the Negro ten dollars.

32

"Come along," said Mr. Whelpley. "If you're going to learn anything about this country, you'd better come along in my plane. It's right up here in the field."

Donald gritted his teeth. The very sight of Mr. Whelpley gave Donald the chills, but Mr. Whelpley had a plane and there was a whole country to see. He might as well accept the invitation.

It was a small, private plane, just big enough for three. The engine was already whirring. The pilot was in the cockpit, waiting for Mr. Whelpley to climb in beside him. Donald, with the honey bear on his shoulder, climbed up a rope ladder into a single cockpit behind.

"What are you going to name him?" called back Mr. Whelpley, buckling on his helmet.

"Oiga," said Donald.

"Oiga! Ridiculous! Do you know what that means?"

"No."

"It's the Spanish word to use when you're calling somebody. It just means *Hey!*"

"I don't care. I like it. His name's Oiga."

"Hmmpf!" snorted Mr. Whelpley.

"Krrrrp!" coughed the engine. The propeller

kicked around faster. They taxied to the end of the field. The plane turned around and the pilot let it thunder back down the field. In a moment they were skimming over the tops of palm trees.

Even with Mr. Whelpley, it was wonderful! They flew over tangled jungles, and over neat fields of tobacco, sugar cane, and corn. They flew low over broad plantations of cocoa and cotton; they flew high over bleak, jagged mountains, famous all over the world for their rich deposits of emeralds, platinum, and gold. Donald looked down from his cockpit and saw everything.

Then they left the plane and went down the great Magdalena River in a dozen different sorts of boats. They traveled in barges, in stern-wheeled steamers, and in square-sailed canoes. On all this long trip north toward the Caribbean Sea, Mr. Whelpley kept munching green gumdrops and talking about the great Latin American hero, Simon Bolivar.

"I suppose you never heard of him," said Mr. Whelpley. "Some people, I dare say, have never heard of George Washington."

"Certainly I've heard of Bolivar," stammered Donald, trying to think quickly. "He was—er—quite a man, wasn't he?"

"Quite a man!" laughed Mr. Whelpley. "I see you don't know anything about Simon Bolivar. He was the hero of more than two hundred battles, one of the greatest heroes of all time. He was the George Washington not just of one country but of six countries. If it hadn't been for Bolivar, this country, and most of the countries you're going to visit in South America, wouldn't be nations at all. They would still be colonies of Spain."

The next day, when they reached the Caribbean Sea, Mr. Whelpley visited the big banana plantation near Santa Marta, but Donald visited the little country village where Bolivar had died. An amiable Negro guide told thrilling stories of Bolivar's hard fight for freedom. Then he told the sad story of how the great hero, when only forty-seven years old, had come to Santa Marta for a rest, but, already sick with exhaustion, had died suddenly of a serious cold.

The last part of the journey the travelers made on muleback, through coffee plantations and dark, mysterious forests that clung to the sides of steep cliffs.

Finally, they climbed up to a city on a high plateau. It was Bogotá, the capital, with its white, paved streets and modern buildings, its fashionable Colombian aristocrats and Indian natives in colorful woolen ponchos.

"Hmmmm," said Donald, suddenly looking at himself critically. "My clothes are not bright enough for this dazzling city. I must have a new outfit."

In the Indian market place of Bogotá, Donald bought himself a long red poncho, green pants, and a round green derby hat. Over his poncho he strapped a belt embroidered in silver and turquoise beads, and stuck into it a leather-handled hunting knife and a machete.

36

"You look ridiculous!" snorted Mr. Whelpley, when Donald strode into the hotel. "I'm glad it's time to go back to the ship."

The next morning the plane took them back again to the Pacific.

"You'll have to hurry," snapped Mr. Whelpley as they came coasting down over the field at Buenaventura. "The ship's due to sail in a few minutes."

Donald clutched Oiga and started to climb out of the plane; but somehow, his long heavy poncho got all mixed up in the rope ladder. He tripped. Down he crashed. Oiga jumped free, ran across the field, and up to the first comfortable branch of a willow tree, out of Donald's reach.

"Oiga!" shouted Donald, trying to kick himself free. "Quick, Mr. Whelpley, get Oiga!"

"I'm through with you and your nonsensical bear toc!" roared Mr. Whelpley, without even turning around. He strode off alone toward the ship.

"That's gratitude for you!" sighed Donald. He drew out his hunting knife and slashed himself free of the tangle of rope. "Oiga!" He ran to the willow tree and shook it. Oiga was asleep!

A shrill whistle pierced the air—the ship's whistle! It was the warning to hurry on board!

37

"Jeepers!" cried Donald. "There must be *something* that will wake up Oiga!" Suddenly he remembered—carnations! Just then, quite close by, he saw a little girl with a white carnation in her hair. Donald grabbed it. He stuck it on a long stick and shoved it under Oiga's nose.

The trick worked to perfection. In another moment, Oiga was on Donald's shoulder again.

The run back to the ship was the fastest that Donald ever made. The townspeople were all at the pier, waving good-by to the passengers.

"*Adiós, amigos!*" panted Donald, as he triumphantly climbed up on board. He smiled and bowed. The people waved their handkerchiefs; Oiga, perched on Donald's shoulder, waved his long, thin tail.

As the ship glided slowly away into the tropical twilight, Donald was suddenly aware of someone standing at his elbow. It was Caspar, his room steward. Something seemed to be troubling him. "If you'll pardon my suggestion, sir," he said timidly, "you should have an especially good sleep tonight."

"Tonight? Why tonight?"

"Tomorrow we cross the equator," answered Caspar. "It is customary for Father Neptune to come aboard then. He always makes it very difficult for a person entering the southern seas for the first time."

"Difficult? What do you mean, difficult?"

"I'm not allowed to say, sir, but you must try to be brave." Caspar looked at Donald mysteriously and hurried off into the darkness.

"Father Neptune!" mused Donald as he went below to his cabin. "What rubbish is that?" He was positive that he wasn't the least bit afraid; nevertheless, for some peculiar reason, he did not sleep very well that night.

CHAPTER VI

Father Neptune's Court

A piece of yellow paper slithered under the door of Donald's cabin. Footsteps scurried away.

Donald leaped out of bed and grabbed the paper. He read:

Neophyte Donald Duck:

"Neophyte? What's that?" He read on: *You are hereby solemnly warned by the Almighty Court of Neptune, Ruler of the Mysterious Deep, to appear at this Court, suitably attired, to hear the charges against you—*

"Charges against me!" cried Donald. His knees felt a little weak. He sank down on his bunk and read on: *Be prepared, O Unfortunate Neophyte, to hear the worst. Contemplate your sins until Neptune's Police come to guide you to your fate.*

(signed) *Neptune, Rex*

"Neptune's Police? What are they talking about?" Donald rang for Caspar. He could not wait. He held his finger on the bell. Caspar came running, breathless, buttoning his white coat as he came in the door.

40

Donald shoved the paper at him. "What does this mean? *Neophyte Donald Duck*. Is that me?"

"Yes, sir. Neophyte means 'first-timer.'"

"But I haven't done anything. They can't do anything to me!"

Caspar looked very solemn. "We're about to cross the equator. I'm afraid it will go hard with you, sir."

Donald was getting nowhere with Caspar. He jumped into his clothes and ran up to the deck for some fresh air. But it certainly was not a cheerful morning. Passengers in their deck chairs whispered as Donald promenaded by, "Is he one?" "Yes, he—" "Do you think they'll give him the works?"

Donald hurried away to the sports deck. At least he could have fun there. But the tennis net was down.

"No sports crossing the equator," said the sports steward. "Got to get ready for the Court."

There was absolutely nothing to do. Donald went back to his cabin and read the yellow document again. *You are warned to appear at this Court, suitably attired.*

"Hmmm," thought Donald. "'Suitably attired.' What's that?" He brushed his teeth; he took a shower; he dried himself off with all the six bath towels hanging on the rack; he put on his best clothes.

Somebody was coming down the corridor—two somebodies! They knocked with three loud raps. "Open in the name of Neptune's Police!"

Donald opened the door just a crack. Neptune's Police! There were two enormous men in white sailor suits with cheeks painted bright red, long false red whiskers, and horns on their heads. They grabbed Donald, rushed him to the deck, and off to Court.

The Court was on the broad stern deck, beside the swimming pool. Beyond the springboard sat Neptune in a white robe, on an oilcloth-draped throne. He wore a crown and white whiskers. With one hand he was clutching a tall trident.

Police were bringing down other passengers and lining them up in a row facing the throne.

"Hmmm," thought Donald. "They must be first-timers, too."

He did not think they were "suitably attired"; they were all in bathing suits.

"Are the guilty ones all here?" bellowed Neptune.

"All here, Your Royal Majesty," answered the Police, bowing very low and stepping up before him.

"Then let the Court proceed!" ordered Neptune, pounding on the deck with his trident. "Prosecutor, commence the prosecution!"

A thin man with black whiskers, black horns, and wearing a skintight black suit, stepped forward from somewhere behind the throne. He unrolled a long white scroll, then looked severely up and down the row of passengers, particularly at Donald.

He cleared his throat. "Police, affix the blindfolds. I am ready to proceed."

Donald's head was jerked back, and a heavy hand-kerchief was tied tight over his eyes.

"Miss Mary Frances Elizabeth Doolittle," the prosecutor's voice began, "step up before the throne."

"This woman looks very guilty," rumbled the voice of Neptune. "With what does the Court charge her?"

"With beclouding the air of your kingdom with her silly, idle chatter."

"Let her be punished!" roared Neptune.

There was suddenly a terrible commotion, a sound of spanking and squealing. Donald managed to lift up his handkerchief. He saw Miss Mary Frances Elizabeth Doolittle go hurtling through the air, up over the pool. Splash! She hit the water, went down, and then came bobbing up again, giggling, and gulping huge mouthfuls of salt water.

"Mr. John Augustus Van Rentlaw, Jr.," shouted the prosecutor, above the laughter of the other passengers. "Step up! Hear the charges against you!"

A policeman caught Donald peeking. Slap! went the handkerchief back down over his eyes.

"I charge you," the prosecutor was saying, "with snoring out loud in your deck chair."

"Guilty!" roared Neptune.

"Guilty!" echoed all the passengers. "Let Neptune's barber give him a shave!"

Again the same terrible commotion!

"Donald Duck!" the prosecutor was calling.

Now at last the policeman ripped the handkerchief off. Donald strode up to the throne.

"I'd say he looks more guilty than all the others," bellowed Neptune. "Read me the charges."

"The Court charges you, Donald Duck—" The prosecutor glared and shook the long scroll right in Donald's face—"with eating twenty times as much as you should for every breakfast, dinner, lunch, and tea. The Court charges you with frightening pretty little Rebecca Jones by swallowing ping-pong balls." He gasped. "Your Royal Majesty, this is the guiltiest sinner of them all."

"Guilty! Guiltiest of them all!" fumed Neptune.

"Guilty! Let him have it!" shouted the crew and all the passengers, too.

"Give him the works!" yelled a louder, single voice from somewhere off in the crowd. It was the voice of Mr. Whelpley. Donald could not mistake it.

One policeman seized Donald by the arms; another grabbed his feet. They carried him right to the barber's chair. Slosh! A big paint brush, dripping with sickly flour paste, slapped him on both cheeks. Then they dragged him from the chair and stretched him flat on his back on a table. They massaged his arms and legs with three kinds of nasty, sticky, fishy jelly.

"Enough!" ordered Neptune. "Throw him to the executioner!"

They yanked Donald to the springboard, out to the very end. They set him down on the ducking stool.

46

"Away with him!" commanded Neptune.

The executioner jerked a rope. Down shot Donald to the very bottom of the pool.

It might all have ended well, but just as Donald gurgled up to the surface, choking with salt water, he sighted Mr. Whelpley, in his pale blue sports jacket and striped flannel pants, leaning over the edge of the pool.

"Are you all right, old man?" grinned Mr. Whelpley.

Donald simply could not stand it. He gave a tremendous push with his feet, lunged into the air, and tackled Mr. Whelpley around the knees. Down under the water they plunged together, kicking and struggling and coughing out great mouthfuls of salty water.

The passengers had never seen anything like it. They leaned over the edge of the pool to get closer, and some of them fell in.

The purser came rushing up to see what it was all about. He skidded, lost his balance, and toppled in. Then the assistant purser jumped in; then the first officer, the second officer, the chief engineer, and the ship's trained nurse in a starched white cap.

Then all of a sudden the Captain appeared, and he jumped in too.

When Donald came to, he was in the doctor's cabin. He was lying on a table and was bandaged from head to foot with adhesive tape and splints. In his hand was a diploma, tied with a red satin bow.

Caspar was hovering over Donald, looking very much worried. "Are you sure you're all right, sir? You've had a terrible time!"

"Terrible?" chortled Donald. "Go take a look at Mr. Whelpley! It's the best fun I ever had!"

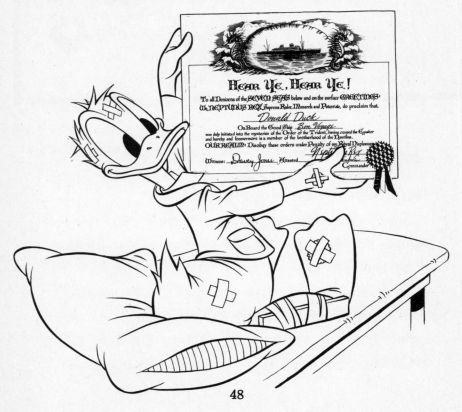

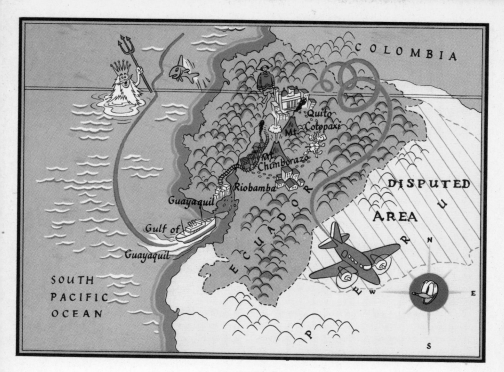

CHAPTER VII

Ecuador—Land of the Equator

Donald was waiting impatiently at the station at Guayaquil when the train for Quito came puffing out of the woods.

The confusion on the platform was deafening. There were families of Negroes in bright shirts and bandanas; they had big fancy baskets of melons and nuts, long loaves of bread, and glassy-eyed fish.

There were Indian families, too, wrapped in gay woolen ponchos and bright-colored shawls. Handsome, stylish Ecuadoreans struggled to get through the mob.

The conductor's whistle blew. Everyone pushed and crowded his way aboard.

"Hey!" Donald stood on tiptoe and looked everywhere, but there wasn't a porter in sight.

There was another last-minute blast from the conductor's whistle. The brakeman waved his flag. The wheels on the little engine screeched and began to turn.

"Porter! Porter!" yelled Donald.

But nobody paid any attention. The passengers were too busy leaning out of the train windows, kissing their friends good-by. The train was chugging out. And Donald was still at the station, in the midst of his big bags, his little bags, Oiga, his golf clubs, and the fourteen Panama hats he had bought in Guayaquil that morning.

Suddenly a tall young Indian appeared on the back platform of the car at the tail end of the train.

"Maybe he'll help me!" thought Donald, picking up a bag and hurling it to him. The Indian saw it coming and caught it, just like a football. Donald

50

hurled another, and still another. One after the other the Indian caught them, and leaned over the rail for more.

The train was picking up speed. Donald threw faster and faster. The crowds on the station platform trembled as the suitcases, hatboxes, and golf clubs whizzed over their heads toward the disappearing train.

"Wait for me! I'm coming too!" cried Donald, racing pell-mell down the middle of the track, dragging his polo sticks and skis.

It was nip and tuck, but Donald made it. He stretched, and snatched at the bars of the back railing, and the Indian hauled him up. The only casualty was Oiga. In the midst of the hubbub, he had escaped and disappeared into the thick, green jungle beside the track.

Donald flopped down limp among his bags, breathless and broken-hearted. Oiga was gone, all because he couldn't speak Spanish to a porter!

The Indian looked down silently, waiting for Donald to catch his breath.

"Thank you," mumbled Donald sadly.

"Don't mention it," said the Indian in perfect English, starting to go back into the train.

51

"You speak English!" Donald's eyes popped open so wide with surprise that a cinder flew into his left eye. Donald clapped his hand over it, and with his right eye he looked the· Indian over. The Indian had on a shirt embroidered in red flowers, and the braids of black hair that hung over his shoulders were tied with red strings. "Hmmm," said Donald. "If you speak English, you must be a North American Indian."

"No," said the Indian. "I am a South American from Ecuador. My language is Spanish, but I study English at the university in Quito."

The train was going quite fast now, and the engine was whistling so much that it was very hard to hear anyone speak. "It's certainly good English, all right," shouted Donald. "And the way you caught my golf clubs! That was something!"

"Nothing at all," answered the Indian. "I play football, left halfback. I've played all over the countries of South America. Guess you'd better go inside and find a place to sit down."

Donald had cinders in both eyes now and could hardly see at all. The Indian helped him carry his things and led him inside to a seat.

"Phew, it's hot!" gasped Donald, rubbing both

eyes with both fists. "Hottest place that I've ever been in."

"On the equator, at sea level, it is always so," said the Indian. "But when you get to Quito, nine thousand feet up, you'll be glad you have a coat."

"Look, look!" cried Donald, his smarting eyes opening wide to stare through the window. On a path just beside the train track a man was calmly walking along, balancing on one shoulder an enormous tree trunk. It must have been three feet thick and almost twenty feet long. "But it's not possible," insisted Donald, "not even in the circus!"

The Indian laughed. He was not at all surprised.

"It's a balsa tree," he said. "It's lighter than cork. Here in Ecuador we grow the best balsa in the world, and we ship it to your country for you to make into life belts, rafts, refrigerator walls, and model airplanes."

As the train sped on, Donald squinted at the dense vegetation outside. In some places the jungle had been cut away and tidy little fields of rice and sugar cane were growing. Sometimes for miles and miles the train skirted the edges of vast cocoa plantations. Every now and then it came to a sudden, jerky stop at some little village of straw-roofed wooden shacks. Here the passengers got out and bought presents for Donald. They gave him delicious little red Ecuadorean bananas, and sweet white pineapple, the same kind he had eaten with the Captain while going through the Canal. The cinders in Donald's eyes had made everyone very sympathetic and friendly.

The air began to feel cooler. The train was climbing toward the mountains. By now all the Negroes had gone; only the Indians and the Ecuadoreans were left. Donald pulled his overcoat over his knees and closed his eyes. No use rubbing them any more. In a moment he fell asleep.

Donald must have slept for a long, long time.

When he woke up, the country outside the window had changed completely. It was bleak, brown, and rocky. The engine was panting. The train was zig-zagging jerkily up around a mountain.

Up and up and around it went. Donald looked down on a curling, twisted ribbon of track. All of a sudden, the train stopped at an Indian village, sur-rounded by snow-capped peaks. The Indians at the station wore enormous white fur pants and ponchos of every imaginable color. They were handsome, sturdy, and broad-chested; the brilliant sun and pure mountain air had made them very strong.

Donald stepped off the train to have his new friend remove the cinders from his eyes. The Indian was leaving the train there.

The air was crisp and cold, and Donald shivered so that the Indian could not get at the cinders. Finally he took Donald into the tiny station.

In a few minutes the cinders were gone—but so were the train and the baggage. "A fine how-do-you-do!" said Donald. He stared forlornly at the spiral of gray smoke curling up the side of the mountain, around which the train had already disappeared.

"And not another train for three days," said the Indian. "I'm afraid you'll have to find something else to ride. It would be a long, long walk to Quito."

Donald thanked the Indian for getting the cinders out. Then he went to the animal market, bought himself a donkey, and started off again. The trail went across a long, lonely plateau to Riobamba, then uphill along slopes that rose up to snowcaps — to the great Andean volcanoes Cotopaxi and Chimborazo. The trail went downhill, through Indian villages, herds of grazing cattle, and beautiful fields of wheat and corn.

Donald rode all the way to Quito and tied his dusty donkey at the door of the Grand Hotel. "I want a room high up, with a balcony," said Donald, "so I can see everything."

"We have such a room," said the smiling proprietor, bowing from the waist. "It looks out on eleven snow mountains, the bishop's palace, the homes of the foreign ambassadors, the park, the shops in the arcade, the football field, and the bull-fighting ring."

"I'll take it," said Donald.

"Sorry, sir," said the proprietor. "That room is reserved for *El Presidente de la Comisión de la América Latina.*"

They gave Donald a small, inside room on a court.

Just walking around in the street in Quito was like walking around on the stage in a play. The houses were pink, pale blue, and yellow, with heavy roofs of reddish-orange tile; they jutted out at absurdly sharp angles.

The people wore strange, unbelievable costumes, and worked at their jobs right out in the street. Indians, sitting cross-legged on the cobblestone pavement, were soling shoes, hammering silver bracelets, weaving straw hats, or frying thick, juicy sausages. Indian women fed their babies, dressed their children, and combed their black hair in the street, the

57

market place, and even in the big square in front of the cathedral. Gaily dressed Indians and white Ecuadoreans in modern clothes walked and shopped and entered the church together.

Donald snapped so many pictures with his camera that he blistered his thumb. Then he went to the market place and snapped five hundred more.

It was a large open-air market where you could buy anything, from an onion to a gold spoon or a hive of buzzing bees. Rows of Indian women in full skirts, sitting along the gutter, offered their wares of rice, corn meal, and raw sweetbreads. You could buy cocoa beans, coffee beans, lima beans, and jelly beans.

You could even buy a trained flea in a red satin cage.

From an Indian in white fur pants, Donald bought a wooden trunk. It was covered inside with flowered wallpaper. Outside it had strips of red-painted metal and now and then a strip of gray fur. It was the fanciest trunk Donald had ever seen, and he filled it with the things he saw the Indians making: a tortoise-shell belt, a set of chessmen that they carved for him out of ivory nuts, an orange-colored poncho, fur pants, and half a dozen pink felt hats.

The Indian who had sold Donald the trunk insisted on carrying it on his back all the way to Donald's

hotel room. Donald wanted to pay him for the trip, but the man would not take any money.

"If only I could say 'thank you' in Spanish!" sighed Donald. "I guess the only thing to do is to give him a present." Donald offered the Indian his gloves, his overcoat, some underdrawers, the telephone book, a toothbrush, the clock on the mantel.

But the Indian just shook his head. He would not take a thing.

"Hmmm," thought Donald, "if I can't say 'thank you,' and he won't take a present, I'll have to do something for him." So Donald took his new friend to a football game.

It was a great game. Now the Indian felt he ought to do something for Donald. He took Donald home to dinner.

They ate a wonderful stew made of goat meat and beans. Then Donald felt he ought to do something for the Indian. Donald took him to the movies.

The Indian thought the show was simply marvelous. Now he felt he ought to do something for Donald. He took Donald to a fancy funeral procession, with six black horses harnessed with flowers, and twelve footmen in tight white pants, shiny patent leather boots, and tall pointed black hats.

They might have gone on doing things for each other forever. But just as they were figuring out who would do what next for whom, the hotel proprietor rushed up, all out of breath. "Telegram, *señor!* We've been looking for you everywhere." He handed it to Donald.

Donald tore it open and read aloud:

Donald Duck,
  Grand Hotel,
   Quito, Ecuador:
Newspapers report you will visit Peru. Would be honored to have you join us in condor hunt. Take plane immediately to Hacienda Waco.

Pedro, Alberto, and Naldo Lopez

"Condor hunt! Jiminy!" cried Donald. "But *Hacienda Waco*, what does that mean?"

"*Waco* is the name of the hacienda; *hacienda* means plantation. You've never heard of it?" The hotel proprietor looked at Donald scornfully, the way Mr. Whelpley always did. "Why, it's the largest and oldest sugar plantation in all Peru!"

"Mmmm, mmmm! Am I lucky!" Donald rushed back to the hotel and wired the Lopez family that he would leave Quito by plane the very next day.

61

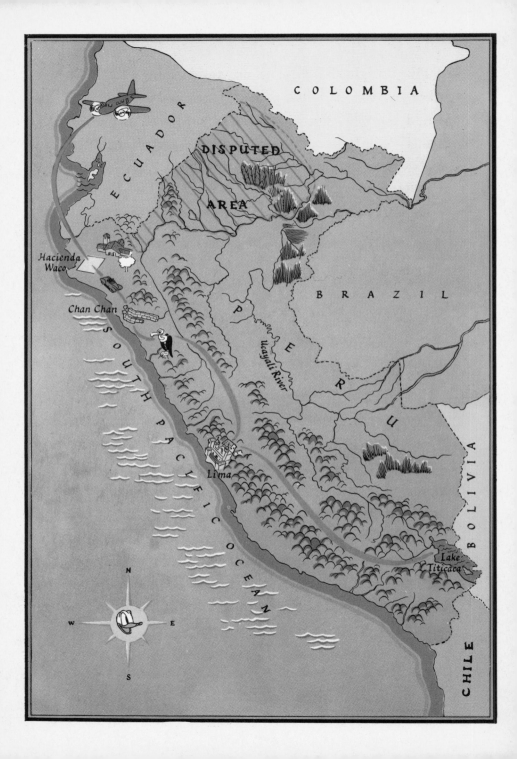

CHAPTER VIII

Catching a Condor in Peru

Down from the mountains of Ecuador Donald flew to the seacoast of northern Peru. It was late at night when Donald's plane dropped him off in the middle of a cleared field of sugar cane at the Hacienda Waco.

"I'll take your bags and show you to the guest house, sir. I'm Paulo, the butler," said a voice from somewhere in the blackness. "Everyone's asleep."

Donald followed Paulo across the field to a dirt road where two horses were waiting.

They rode in the dark for almost an hour, on and on, through endless fields of sugar cane. At last they arrived at a group of low white buildings, built in the form of a square. In front of one they dismounted, and Paulo opened the door.

Donald stepped into a sitting room lavishly decorated with tapestries, oil paintings, and furniture upholstered in rich red brocade. On one wall was a long cabinet of rifles, shotguns, and enormous old-fashioned revolvers. The whole room glittered with silver ornaments, silver bowls, and silver chests.

Paulo began unpacking Donald's clothes and hanging them up in a massive wardrobe with carvings of Spanish warriors on the doors. "I expect you're quite tired, sir," he said. "I'll prepare the bed."

Donald got into his pajamas and followed Paulo through the bedroom door. "Some bed!" gasped Donald. Six people could have slept in it comfortably. It had heavy arched head- and footboards of carved black ebony, inlaid with intricate patterns in ivory, silver, and gold. It had a roof, with a long canopy of mosquito netting drooping down to the floor.

"Now I'd advise you to sleep, sir," said Paulo. "The condor hunt starts at quarter past dawn."

He snapped off the light and disappeared.

A bugle sounded somewhere outside. Donald leaped up and hurried into his hunting clothes.

His hosts had already loaded a car with hunting equipment, and were waiting outside the guest house to greet him. They were three handsome Peruvians in riding boots and felt sombreros.

"We are honored with your presence, *Señor* Donald," said one. "I'm Pedro. This is Alberto, and this is Naldo."

They all shook hands and jumped into the car. The

floor of the back seat was piled high with wooden stakes, rolls of chicken wire, high-powered rifles, coils of thick rope, and big hunks of raw meat.

"Did you ever hunt condors before?" asked Naldo, as they drove off. "Around here, it's considered a duty. The condors are snatching the farmers' pigs."

Donald tried to recall what a condor looked like. He did not intend to let these Peruvians think there was anything about hunting that he did not know. "I've hunted everything," he bragged, "brown bears, black bears, cinnamon bears, and grizzly bears; wallabies and bearded gnus, and many a condor."

"Do you shoot them, or lasso them while they're sleeping?" asked Naldo in breathless admiration.

Donald felt very cocky. "Oh, I prefer to lasso them while they're awake."

"Never heard of such a thing!" exclaimed Naldo. "After all, the condor is one of the largest, most ferocious birds in the world."

"So condors are birds," thought Donald. This was serious. Lassoing a bird would be quite a trick.

The country was getting barren. The road had ended, and they were driving across open plains on rough, uneven sand toward an enormous mass of ruins. It looked like a whole city of brown baked clay.

"Let the condors wait a minute," said Pedro. "We ought to show *Señor* Donald the sights on the way."

They stopped. Pedro and Donald wandered in and out among the maze of roofless, deserted walls. Nothing was living except a few hungry wasps; not even a vine or bramble could find water there.

"Hundreds of years ago, before the empire of the Incas, this was the wealthy city of Chan Chan," said Pedro.

He led Donald toward a deep pit, a few hundred yards away, where some Indian workmen were digging. There, in the earth right in front of them, lay an Indian mummy, half dug out of the brownish sand. Donald jumped down into the hole. Scattered here and there were painted earthen bowls, jugs, turquoise-colored stones, and bits of brittle cloth.

Pedro motioned to one of the workmen to hand Donald his shovel. "Go ahead. Dig around a bit. Dig up something for yourself."

Donald poked and dug. The shovel hit something hard, a black jug with two funny lobsters carved on the spout. "Well!" said Donald. "Who'd put a thing like that down here?"

"The Chimus," said Pedro. "They were Indians who lived here in Chan Chan before the Incas, and this, we've just discovered, was one of their burial grounds. This Chimu here," he pointed to the mummy, "was probably a fisherman. That's why they buried him with a jug with a lobster design. Incidentally, a burial jug like that is called a *waco*. We've found so many all around here that we named the plantation *Hacienda Waco*."

The shouting of Naldo and Alberto resounded through the pit. "If you expect to catch a condor, you'd better come soon."

Pedro dragged Donald, still clutching his *waco*, up out of the pit and back to the car.

67

As they drove on, the coast grew more and more lonely and barren. Now they were jogging right along by the side of the steel-gray sea. Desolate, colorless cliffs rose up through the distant mists. Flocks of pelicans, wild cranes, and guano birds swooped down over the sand, piercing the air with their squawks.

Donald shivered. "Funny how cold it is here."

"It's always like this here," said Alberto, "from Chile to Ecuador. It's because of the cold Humboldt Current that flows up from the Antarctic. For hundreds of miles there's nothing but sand and rock desert."

"Look!" cried Naldo.

Alberto jammed on the brakes. Far up the beach, at the foot of a jagged cliff, a tall black something, larger than a man, was jumping among the boulders.

The Peruvians grabbed their guns, the stakes, the wire, and a large hunk of mutton and ran ahead down the beach, motioning to Donald to stay back.

The black creature disappeared.

Stealthily, the Peruvians tiptoed forward. On a level space between two boulders, quickly and expertly, they erected a fence. Right in the middle of it they dropped the meat. Then they tiptoed back to Donald, and all lay down flat on their faces.

"When the condor lands inside that fence to get the meat, he'll be trapped," whispered Pedro. "A condor can't take off again from a little space."

They waited, but the black creature did not reappear.

Donald raised himself up on one elbow. This kind of hunting did not suit him at all. The sand was hard and cold.

"Maybe the condor doesn't see the meat; you ought to show him," he said impatiently.

"Shhhhhh!" The brothers raised their eyebrows.

Donald thought of all the imaginary bears he had

caught on his imaginary hunts. He had never waited
for an animal to come to him. Of course not!

"Gentlemen," he said, suddenly leaping to his
feet, "enough of this dillydallying. If you please,
a pork chop and my lasso!"

Donald seized the chop and a coil of rope and raced
up the beach. Way up on the edge of the cliff,
above the boulders, a dusky shadow darkened
the gray rock. Donald ran on farther. Then he
stopped and gaped, as he caught full sight of the
evil-looking, black-feathered monster lounging up
there above him.

"This meat business is silly," Donald said to
himself. He stuck the pork chop in his pocket.
"I'll simply lasso him right there, pull him down,
and carry him off on my back."

Noiselessly, Donald shinnied up the steep, jagged
crag. The condor did not see him; he did not flutter
a feather. The white ruff around the base of his
neck made a perfect target. Donald coiled the rope
and slung it. It caught. He yanked it. What a
cinch! He had the creature right there in a noose.
He hauled back the rope, hand over hand.

Faster and still faster he kept on hauling, until
suddenly he heard a thunderous flapping. He looked

up, expecting to see the condor coming down. But the condor was going up and Donald was going up, too! Hanging to the rope tied fast to the condor's thick neck, Donald went dangling over the crags.

Donald shrieked to his Peruvian companions, far below him on the beach: "Do something quick!" They could not even hear. They thought it was some new-fangled trick in condor hunting; they cheered and threw their hats in the air.

Higher and still higher the bird and the dangling Donald sailed on. Suddenly Donald remembered the pork chop in his pocket.

With his right hand he gripped the rope, and with his left he seized the chop. He brandished it, so that the condor could take a long, hungry look. Then, with careful aim, he flung it. Plop! It fell right on top of the big chunk of mutton inside the little wooden condor-catching fence.

The strategy worked like a charm. The condor's greedy eyes followed the careening chop as it plunged to earth; they sighted the tasty, raw meat so invitingly waiting there below.

Donald's sky tour was over. The bird was flying his passenger down! Just above the ground Donald let go the rope, jumped, and landed on both feet

outside the fence. Right behind him, the condor swooped down to a perfect landing inside the fence.

"Bravo!" shouted the Peruvians, throwing their arms around Donald and slapping him on the back. Leaving Pedro to dispose of the vicious condor, Alberto and Naldo carried Donald off down the beach on their shoulders.

"Magnificent! Never saw anything like it!" Naldo kept saying. "Who in the world taught you to catch condors like that?"

"I don't exactly remember," chuckled Donald, "but I think it may have been my old friend, *El Presidente de la Comisión de la América Latina.*"

CHAPTER IX

One Day for Lima

On reaching Lima, Donald strode through the lobby of the Hotel Bolivar. By the tourist shop, just inside the front door, hung a sign: ENGLISH-SPEAKING GUIDES.

"I'll take one," said Donald.

A short, dark-skinned Peruvian in a black felt hat appeared from somewhere inside.

"Show me the town," said Donald, hurrying ahead of him out to the street.

73

"First, we have coffee," said the guide. "Then, we make plans. Today, maybe we see Spanish churches. Tomorrow—"

"No tomorrow!" interrupted Donald crossly. "I have one day, today!"

"One day for Lima!" The guide's eyes bulged in amazement. "Lima—City of Kings! City of Pizarro! *Señor*, you are the type who would spare but one short week end for Heaven! Lima in one day! It is impossible!" He threw up his hands and started to walk off, but Donald grabbed him.

"You take me to see everything! Now!"

Those were the last words that Donald had breath enough to speak out loud that day.

The guide took a firm grip on his arm, and off they started at a trot through the Plaza de Congreso, the governor's palace, the Chamber of Deputies, and the Senate. They raced through parks, in and out of forty old Spanish churches, eleven monasteries, the botanical gardens, flea market, and zoo.

Donald wanted to stop and look at the boa constrictor, but the guide pulled him on. "No time," he kept saying, "no time to look. If you stop to look at anything, you won't see everything."

They whirled along through the ancient halls of

74

the university. "Oldest college in all the Americas," panted the guide, "built in 1551." They whizzed past the Casa de Moneda, Spanish name for the mint, where workers sat at long benches, making beautiful Peruvian coins. They flew to the Jockey Club and out along a wide boulevard to the ancient jail. "Notice the super-luxurious cells," the guide whispered weakly, "for criminals of distinction and fame."

Hour after hour, on and on they raced. Sometimes they brushed past beautiful, aristocratic Peruvian ladies, shopping in the fashionable shops under the arcades.

Round the bull ring they went. Past the railway that twisted up sixteen thousand feet through the bare, bleak Andes to the world's most famous copper mine! To the fine modern airport! Pell-mell, lickety-split past the Church of the Shoeless Monks! To the Torre-Tagle Palace, the most magnificent old Spanish mansion in all Peru! Donald stared breathlessly at the delicate carving of the doorways and the brilliant colors of the marble floors.

They hurried to the museum to see the historical remains of ancient Peru. There were shelves filled with hundreds of *wacos* like the one Donald had

75

dug up, all painted with pictures of birds, animals, and funny bearded men. There were exquisitely woven rugs, gold necklaces, and polished earthen ornaments made by the many tribes of artistic Indians who ruled Peru before the Spaniards came. A whole room was filled with relics of Pizarro, portraits of Pizarro, pistols of Pizarro, gauntlets and garters of Pizarro, documents of Pizarro, and drawings of Pizarro conquering and murdering all the fine old Indians of Peru.

The day was almost over. Donald could hardly push himself along.

"Pizarro," whispered the guide feebly, gasping out one word at a time, "built . . . all Lima . . . but Pizarro . . . make . . . too much . . . murder. Pizarro bad. . . . murder so many people . . . Soon . . . people . . . murder Pizarro. Too bad Pizarro . . . so bad!" The guide's knees seemed to be folding up. He was sinking down in a crumpled heap on the pavement in front of the cathedral. Then suddenly his arms and legs spread out limply, and he rolled over flat on his back. "One day for Lima!" he mumbled dolefully as he fell asleep.

CHAPTER X

Boats and Llamas in Bolivia

High up on the Peruvian shore of Lake Titicaca, Donald boarded a big modern steamer to take him across to the Bolivian side.

"This is an amazing ship," the Captain told him proudly.

"It looks like any ship on the sea," said Donald.

"Ah!" said the Captain, "that's just it. This isn't the sea. You must remember that you are on the highest large lake in the world, twelve thousand five hundred feet in the air. To get here, this great ship had to be hauled over the Andes piece by piece. It took forty-six cars in nine trains, hundreds of mules, and llamas by the score. When all the ship's pieces were assembled on the shore of the lake, we fitted them together like a giant jigsaw puzzle."

"Amazing," said Donald.

They were now approaching the Bolivian shore, passing the islands where the Incas had built temples in which to worship the sun and the moon. The ruins of colossal stone arches were still standing, deserted.

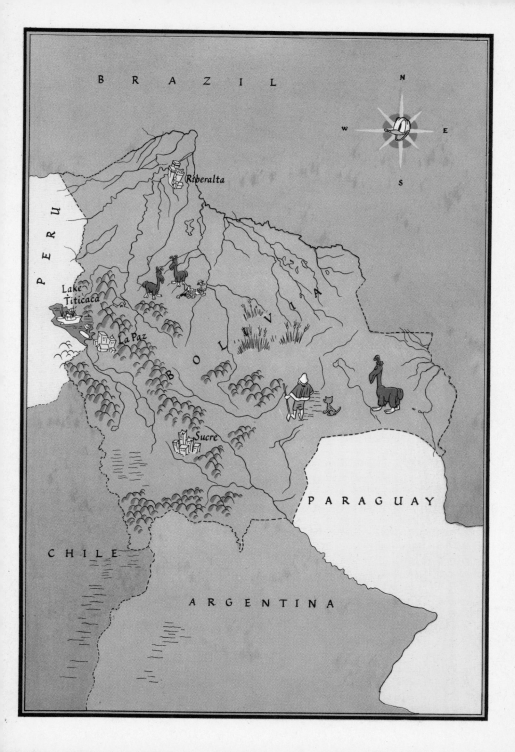

"Did Pizarro kill all the Incas?" asked Donald, as the ship glided slowly in toward the dock.

"No. Pizarro didn't kill the Inca shepherds because he knew they didn't have any gold. Many Bolivian shepherds of today are pure Inca."

"If only I could meet a real Inca!" sighed Donald.

"Come along. That's easily arranged," smiled the Captain.

Donald followed the Captain down the gangway and ashore, into a throng of bright-ponchoed, chattering Indians. The Captain seemed to be looking for someone in particular. He pushed his way toward a huddle of young Indians who were trading bowls of corn, meal, and barley for the fresh fruits and vegetables that had just arrived on the ship. "Coya!" called the Captain suddenly to a dark Indian boy in the middle of the crowd.

Coya turned and came running toward the Captain, carrying a bowl of fresh fruits on his head. The Captain began talking very fast in some language that Donald had never heard before. Coya's sun-tanned face broke into an enormous smile. He beamed, first at the Captain and then at Donald.

"I've arranged for you to visit him," said the Captain to Donald. "Do as he does and you will

80

learn how Inca shepherds live, and have lived for as many years as anyone can remember."

Donald said *adiós* to the Captain and trailed Coya along a rough, narrow path by the side of the lake. After a few minutes they rounded a bend and came upon a little canoe, tied fast to some coarse, heavy grass. It was made entirely of thick brown reeds, all neatly woven and bound together. Even the sail was made of reeds; it hung from a tall reed pole at the bow. Coya motioned for Donald to get in and sit down; then he untied the rope, jumped in himself, and pushed off.

It was a wonderful sail. They headed right into the crisp wind; the little ship tilted to starboard; the spray flew fast. After a while, Coya reached up and rolled up the sail. It was time to fish.

By sunset, when they sailed into shore again, Donald had caught four long, thin, black fish, three round ones, one turtle, and a tree stump.

They beached the canoe and climbed over a rocky hillside up to a high plateau. It was dusk, and the high wall of mountains beyond had turned a solemn, purple gray. Great herds of llama, sheep, and shaggy alpaca were nibbling at the stubby grass between the boulders. Right in the midst of them stood the

little home of Coya. It was built of stones and was covered with a thatched straw roof.

Coya's mother and father welcomed Donald with warm smiles and a bowl of steaming hot mutton, served on a rough stone bench in front of the stove. Donald had never been in such a house before. It was kitchen, bedroom, workshop, and storehouse, all in one room. Through the wide, open doorway, three hens came wandering in, scratching for crumbs.

After dinner, they all sat on woolen blankets on the ground outside and watched the moon come up, while Coya and his father played sad little tunes on their reed flutes. Then everyone went inside to bed.

During Donald's visit, there were many different things to be done, most of which had to do with llamas. Several dozen llamas were shaggy enough to be sheared. There were llama skins to be cut and sewed into leather sandals. There were big sides of llama meat hanging on wooden pegs, ready to be made into stew.

Coya's special job was way off on the hillsides, watching and guarding the herds. He did not have a horn, or even a dog; he could control any llama just by blowing two soft notes on his flute.

"I'd like to boss those silly llamas myself," said

Donald one day, as Coya was playing a little song to call a llama down from the top of a cliff.

That afternoon, while Coya slept in the warm sun, Donald borrowed the flute and practiced; but whenever he tried to pipe *Do Re Mi Fa Sol La Ti Do*, it came out *Do Re Mi Fa Sol Peep Squeak Whew!*

"Exasperating!" grunted Donald, "but the llamas probably won't know the difference." So he offered to lead the herd home.

Donald drew in a deep breath, threw out his chest, and began to play, "Yankee Doo . . . Pshh . . . Peep!" The animals looked scared; they turned away and shied off. Coya roared with laughter.

"Hmmm," thought Donald. "This job requires strategy. It must be my foreign appearance that frightens them. I'll have to keep out of sight."

Donald hid behind a big boulder where the llamas could not see him, but could still hear the sound of his flute. Again he began to pipe.

Suddenly Donald heard the clatter of hoofs just behind him. "Success!" he thought.

Crouching low over the rocks and stubble, Donald ran forward, while the animal clambered along behind. Donald's handsome best hat caught on a bramble bush and stuck there, but Donald did not stop to snatch it back. He kept right on going.

Over the hill and down across the long plateau to Coya's house Donald piped on.

By a different route, Coya had arrived home first and had brought out his parents in front of the house to greet the great piper. Donald pranced up before them, brandishing his flute in the air in triumph. Then he turned to the "herd."

Donald gasped. "Why you—you—you—you're no llama! You're only a foolish scrawny goat!"

The goat looked at him calmly and went on munching something, one end of which was protruding from his bony jaw. "Why, it's my hat!" Donald cried. "My best hat! He's chewed it to ribbons!"

Then, to Donald's own surprise, he joined Coya and his parents in a side-splitting laugh.

With many shakings of hands and smilings and bowings, Donald took leave of the hospitable Bolivian shepherds. He crossed Lake Titicaca again and took the train to the port of Mollendo, Peru, to catch the boat for the Chilean port of Valparaiso.

According to the custom at that rock-bound port, Donald was lowered out of Peru onto the boat in a big wooden chair, on the end of a rope.

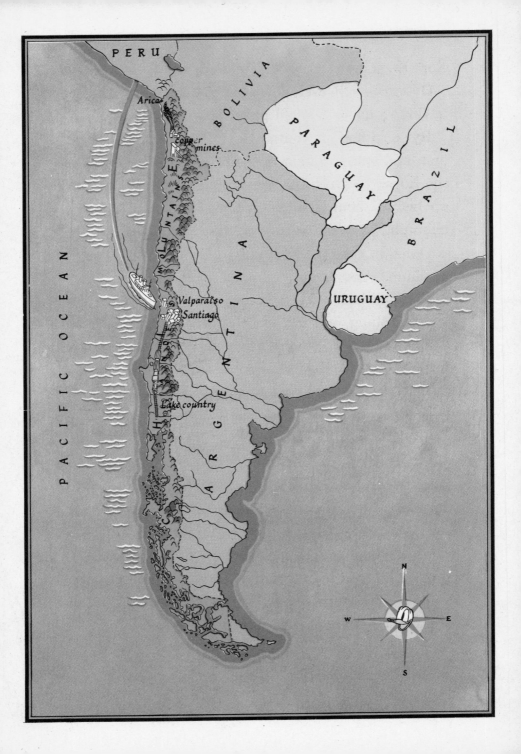

CHAPTER XI

Looking for Lakes in Chile

Tourists milled about in the office of the Prefect of Police in Valparaiso, Chile. Several boats with foreigners had arrived, and all of them had to register immediately with the police.

Donald had just shown his passport and vaccination certificate, and had written his name down in a long, black book. He had not had time to study a single thing about the country, but, with a Chilean flag in his buttonhole, he felt as wise as any native.

"Pardon me, sir," said a voice at his elbow. It belonged to a North American tourist, a wiry little man, wearing pinch-nose glasses, white flannel trousers, a tan-checked flannel jacket, and tan-and-white shoes. "Your face is very familiar. Haven't I seen you somewhere, possibly in California?"

"I dare say," said Donald. "I get around a bit."

"Mmmmm," continued the tourist, eyeing the Chilean flag on Donald's lapel. "I see you're well acquainted with this country."

"Naturally," replied Donald.

"We've just arrived in South America." He handed Donald a calling card:

Mortimer S. Billingsby
Boston, Mass.
President, United Canoe Club of the Americas

"Our club is traveling as a little party," he continued. He pointed to a group of his friends, who were still writing their names in the black book. They all looked somewhat like Mr. Billingsby, and were dressed in the same sort of sport clothes. Under one arm, each one was carrying an enormous bulky package that seemed to be made of gray canvas. "We call ourselves the 'Canoodlers,'" he went on.

"Yes, yes," interrupted Donald impatiently, "but what's in those gray packages?"

"Our folding canoes," answered Mr. Billingsby.

"You're going canoeing down here in Chile?" asked Donald excitedly. "Where?"

"Wherever we can find a lake. Since you know the country, probably you can tell us where to go."

"Certainly," said Donald confidently.

"I was just thinking," continued Mr. Billingsby, "that you might like to team up with us. You could show us around the city a bit, and then lead us off

88

to some faraway, picturesque lake. We would then arrange to make you an Honorary Canoodler."

"It's a deal," said Donald. His heart throbbed with excitement. This looked like a good thing!

Mr. Billingsby beckoned to the other Canoodlers, who came clustering around. "Gentlemen, we are lucky. We have a guide. May I introduce Mr. — ?"

"Donald," said Donald.

The Canoodlers all shook hands with Donald. They beamed at him and all began talking at once.

"Quiet, boys!" interrupted Donald suddenly. "Let's get going."

He strode out through the prefecture door with the fifteen Canoodlers and their fifteen folding canoes following right behind. The main business street along the water front was crowded, but the side streets were empty. These streets went straight up to the cliffs above. Each street had a little cable-car elevator running up and down the middle.

"Just the sort of contraption from which to look around and spot some distant lake," thought Donald. He hustled his party up to one of the elevator cars and herded them all in. Machinery clanked. The motorman slammed the door. Iron gadgets grated and groaned. Slowly the car began

crawling up the cliff. It was a very exciting ride.

The Canoodlers looked out over the city and exclaimed about the wonderful view. On the distant sandy beaches, young Chileans were frisking about. Way, way down the coast they could see the bright flags of the horse-race track at Viña del Mar.

"What a fine city!" said Mr. Billingsby, craning his neck to see it all. "It's built just like an amphitheatre around the bay. And you're a fine guide, Mr. Donald, to have thought of this car."

"I knew you'd like it," said Donald, feeling very much pleased with himself.

Donald kept scanning the hillsides above, hoping suddenly to see the glimmer of some silvery lake.

The green slopes were dotted with lovely Spanish homes with terraced gardens, like many of the homes in California. There were flowering vines and thick groves of stately poplar and eucalyptus trees. Higher up, the hills were covered with neat orchards, but nowhere did Donald see any silvery lake.

"I'll have to take them somewhere else," he thought. "There must be lakes somewhere."

As the little cable car came to the end of the line, to a platform at the top of the hill, Donald saw a large long-distance type bus labeled *Santiago* approaching on the highway. Donald signaled it to stop, and bundled his Canoodlers aboard.

All the way through the lovely Chilean valleys to Santiago, Donald chatted about what he saw. He talked about how much greener the hills were than in Bolivia and Peru, and how few Indians there were. "The trick to this job of being a guide," he thought to himself, "is just to keep your eyes open and explain what you see. I'll just keep talking and traveling till eventually we come to a lake." He felt delightfully important.

In that glamorous Latin American capital, Santiago, according to the Spanish custom, Donald and the Canoodlers promenaded through the fine,

wide streets and plazas. The air was balmy and
delightful; the moon glistened on the peaks of the
Andes that rose in a jagged white wall to the east.

When they sauntered through the Avenida de
las Delicias, with its long row of statues of South
American heroes, Donald lectured on history. The
inscriptions on each monument told Donald all the
facts, but he pretended he had known them all
before. He made a long speech about Bolivar, the
George Washington of the northern part of the
continent; another about O'Higgins, the George
Washington of Chile; and still another about San
Martin, the George Washington of Argentina.

"My!" Mr. Billingsby interrupted suddenly. "What you don't know about South America isn't worth knowing at all!"

If only Mr. Whelpley could have listened to that! Donald puffed out his chest as he had never puffed it out before. Just at that instant, his eye caught sight of a bright-colored poster on the railing of the band-concert stand in the middle of the plaza. "Tourists!" it read. "Chile Has Everything. Go North to Its World-Famous Copper Mines. Go South to Its Wild, Picturesque Lakes."

"Lakes!" gasped Donald. "I knew I'd find some!

We must all leave for the south this very night."

Donald rushed the Canoodlers right back to the hotel and made them pack their bags. He hustled and bustled to get the whole party down to the station to catch the midnight train.

As soon as the train pulled out, Donald went to his compartment and immediately got into bed. He tried to go to sleep quickly so that it would seem only a minute before he would be plunging his canoe paddle into the blue water.

The train's shrill whistle split the air, waking Donald with a start. The brilliant sun beat against the window shade alongside his berth. Donald tried to pull it up, but it stuck so that he could not look out. He hurried into his canoe clothes. The train was already slowing down and chugging into the station.

As Donald strode down the train's little stairway, the Canoodlers were already on the platform in their shorts and sun helmets, waiting to greet him. But it was not the sort of greeting he had expected at all. Shivering and shaking and numb with cold, they glared at him with terrifying scowls. Donald gaped. Billowy snowdrifts blanketed the station. An icy blast of winter wind swept down from the

94

white hillside. The lake was frozen solid, and gay young folk in warm, bright wools were skating merrily upon it. It was August, the wrong season for the United Canoe Club of the Americas to paddle across the Chilean lakes!

But Donald Duck was not the sort of person to be stumped by a mere quirk of the weather. He drew in a deep breath and jumped briskly off the train's bottom step. "My! What a fine cool day!" he called out cheerfully. "We'll put the canoes on skis. Ski canoeing! What fun!"

"F-f-f-f-fun!" roared the fifteen furious, shuddering Canoodlers. They dropped their canoes; in a wild stampede they rushed upon Donald.

Donald ran toward the hills. Up and up through drifts knee-deep, he made for the tallest peak. The angry pursuing Canoodlers soon flopped, bogged down in the soft snow, and gave up the chase.

As Donald trekked back over the mountainous miles to Santiago, he composed a little verse about his adventure in the Chilean lakes:

Chile isn't chilly in the winter. No, it's not.
It's chilly in the summertime, when Chile should
    be hot.

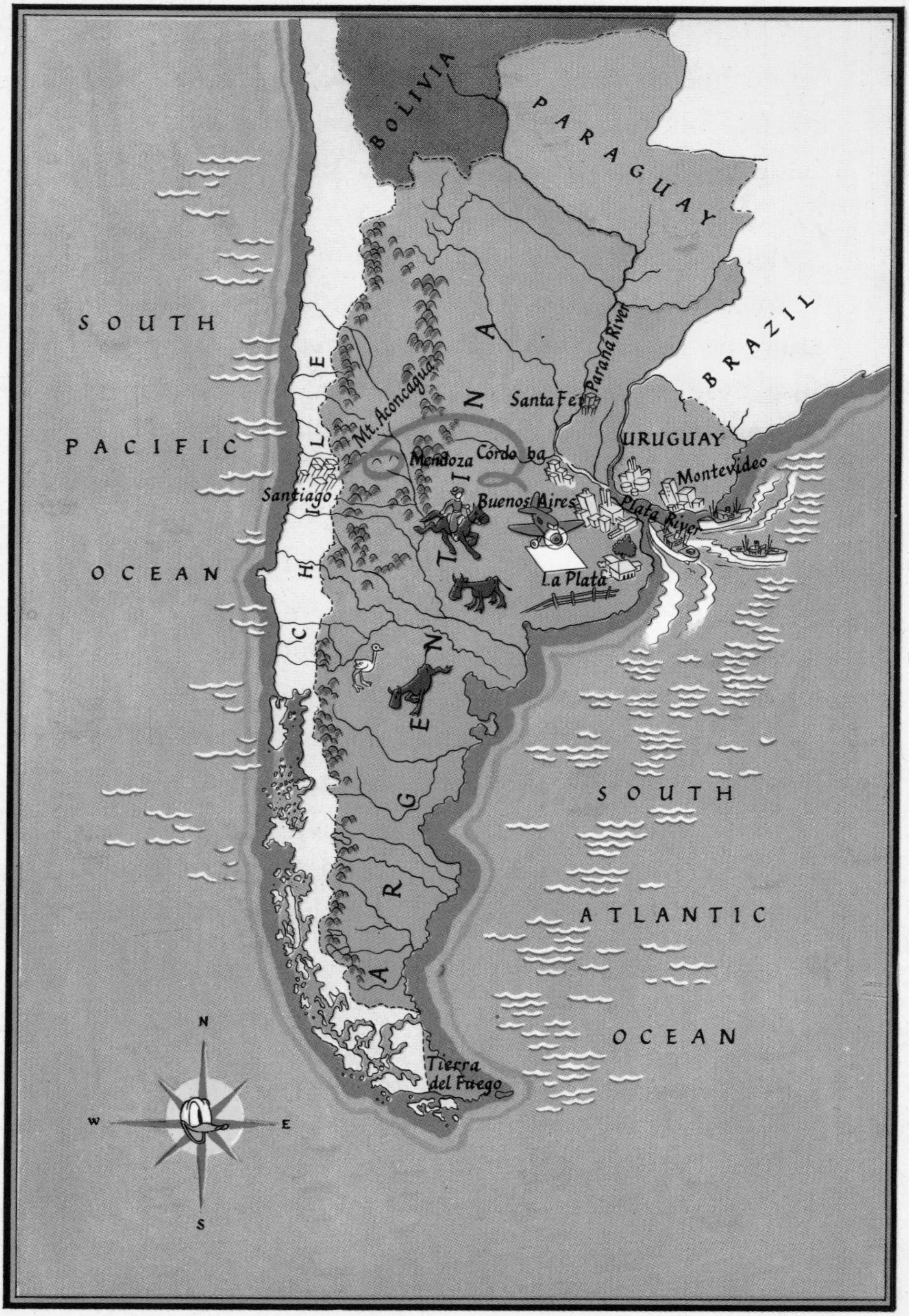

BOLIVIA
PARAGUAY
BRAZIL
URUGUAY
CHILE
ARGENTINA
SOUTH PACIFIC OCEAN
SOUTH ATLANTIC OCEAN
Mt. Aconcagua
Santa Fe
Paraná River
Córdoba
Mendoza
Santiago
Buenos Aires
Montevideo
Plata River
La Plata
Tierra del Fuego
N
S
E
W

CHAPTER XII

Over the Andes to Argentina

At the airport in Santiago Donald once more stood on the ground, shaking his fist at a vanishing passenger plane. "Brrrr! Again he's got my priority!"

"Don't take it so hard, *señor*," said the captain of the airport. "You're not the only one to lose your seat to *El Presidente de la Comisión de la—*"

"That name! Don't repeat it!"

"Excuse me, *señor*. I was only going to say that another passenger, the Argentine heiress, *Señorita* Rosa Cordoba, had to give up her seat too. She has chartered a private plane to fly her to her *estancia—*"

"Her what?" grunted Donald.

"Her *estancia*, her ranch. She has invited you, *señor*, to fly with her as her guest."

"I suppose I have to," growled Donald.

The motors of the little plane were already humming. The pilot, the copilot, and the *señorita* were already strapped in their seats when Donald climbed in. The *señorita's* seat was just ahead of Donald's. She turned, looked at him, and smiled.

Never before in all his life had Donald seen anyone so beautiful. She had enormous black sparkling eyes, wavy licorice-colored hair, and white flashing teeth. She had everything!

Speechless with admiration, Donald flopped in his seat. The plane was off! It circled over the field to gain altitude, then turned its nose east toward the mighty, towering pinnacles, the backbone of the Andes. Higher than all the rest rose the lofty white peak of Mount Aconcagua, the second tallest mountain in the world. Donald stared at the terrifying panorama of desolate crags and felt lonely and sad. Then he stared at the lovely *señorita* and cheered up again. He must think of something clever and start conversation. He cleared his throat, but just then the plane hit an air pocket, and Donald went dumb with fright.

The plane lurched, but caught hold, and once more began to climb. Over the pilot's shoulder, Donald saw the altimeter, the little instrument that showed exactly how high in the air they were— 17,000—up—up—18,000—19,000 feet! The air was getting thinner. The *señorita* was inhaling oxygen from the oxygen tank beside her. Donald watched her dainty nostrils quiver.

"I'll tell her," he thought, "how prettily she sniffs." He tapped her gently on the shoulder. "*Señorita,*" he said boldly, "you're a picture to behold."

She turned and flashed him an uncomprehending smile. "*Pardon . . . no comprendo.*" Then she turned her back again.

Spanish! No English! A fine how-do-you-do!

Donald's heart slumped. All the way over the Andes and down over the flat, treeless plains, the Argentine pampas, Donald sat glumly gazing at the endless fields of wheat and grazing cattle.

At dusk, when the plane landed at the *señorita's estancia* near Buenos Aires, Donald still had thought of no solution. Out in the vast gardens, guests were arriving for the barbecue. But *Señorita* Rosa spoke only Spanish, and Donald felt out in the cold.

"At least," he thought suddenly, "I can look Argentinian." Quickly he borrowed a Gaucho suit: black boots, full green trousers, and a heavy leather girdle studded with gold coins. Then he invited the *señorita* to dance on the polished wooden dance platform in the middle of the garden grass. Ah, her perfume! If only he could tell her how deliciously she smelled of cinnamon sticks!

But Donald was not allowed to dance with her often. A handsome Gaucho always came and led her off, whispering to her in soft syllables of Spanish.

"My brilliant wit! The stories of all my daring adventures!" Donald wailed to himself. "Useless! How can I impress her when I speak no Spanish?"

Donald could not stand this very long. Glumly he settled down to sample the Argentine beefsteak, cooked on a spit in a stone fireplace beside the banquet table. The *señorita* showed him how to eat it in the Gaucho way, holding his bread and meat in one hand, and a big knife in the other. From a silver cup, through a silver sipper, he drank the Argentine *maté*, a sort of tea strange to Donald.

Long into the night, the party went on. The Gauchos, in their magnificent sheepskin saddles, entertained the guests with feats of rough riding on their thoroughbred Arabian steeds. They jumped; they hurdled; they showed how an Argentine captures an ostrich. When Donald tried to show how easily a North American could do that trick, he was tossed into a treetop and had to be helped down with a pole.

Too soon, the evening came to an end.

In the morning, when Donald came down to say

good-by, the *señorita* was already strolling in the garden. She did not wait for him to struggle with words he could not say; she quickly ushered him into a limousine waiting especially for him at the gate, smiled, and waved *adiós*.

Donald lounged back comfortably among the pale green cushions as the car sped off to Buenos Aires. What a car! It had a chauffeur and a footman up in front, dressed in pale green uniforms to match the car. There were red roses in a silver holder clamped on the inside of the door; there was a silver box of chocolate nougats on the arm of the seat. "Such luxury!" thought Donald. "The *señorita* must consider me a visitor of distinction and fame."

They turned into a broad highway that cut like a knife across wide, flat fields of corn and flax.

"Pssst—hello!" said a voice right next to Donald's ear. It came from a little green metal funnel on the end of a speaking tube connected with the front seat. The footman was talking into the other end of the tube. "I say hello," he continued.

"Hello yourself," said Donald.

"I speak English," said the footman. "What is your pleasure?"

"Just show me the sights," said Donald indif-

ferently, not wishing to appear surprised by such
luxury and service. "Show me whatever you usually
show to famous visitors."

The chief sights were the great meat-packing
factories. Donald saw how Argentine beef is tested
and salted and canned. He visited the wharves
along the River Plata where freighters from every
country were loading on beef to take abroad. Then
he visited all sorts of smaller Argentine factories,
hat factories, shoe factories, factories that made

washcloths, and other factories that made nails.

"Argentina has so many factories," complained Donald. "Show me something else."

The footman then took him through all the parks of Buenos Aires, to the horse-race track, the jockey and the yachting clubs. The sport-loving Argentines had sport clubs everywhere. Donald had tea in a little palm-shaded patio inside the beautiful *Casa Rosada*, the Rose House, where the President lived.

Late in the afternoon they drove down the fashionable promenade on the River Plata. "Now you've seen every sight except the best and last of all," said the green-uniformed footman. "We have a unique custom here in Buenos Aires, a way of expressing our gratitude for the honor of entertaining a visitor of great distinction and fame. To enjoy it properly, *señor*, it will be necessary for you to get out of the car."

"Certainly," said Donald, "I'd be glad to." He was trembling with excitement. "A visitor of great distinction and fame," he whispered to himself. "It must be something for me!"

As Donald stepped down from the car to the sidewalk, a vast canopy of brilliant color suddenly fluttered over his head. "Pigeons!" cried Donald.

"What a sight! Fancy pigeons! Painted pigeons!"

"Yes," smiled the footman proudly, "painted, but with a dye not harmful to the pigeon. When a great celebrity visits our city, we paint the pigeons in his national colors."

"My! My!" exclaimed Donald, looking all around at the hundreds of gorgeous birds. "You really mean that every one was painted just for me?"

The footman looked very surprised. "Oh, no, *señor*, not for you. They were painted for a very famous man, *El Presidente de la Comisión*—"

"That man!" shouted Donald, interrupting. "He always steals my place and now he steals my pigeons!"

"Too bad, *señor*," sighed the footman. "But never mind. Perhaps, some day, we will have pigeons painted even for you." He clicked his heels, bowed, jumped back in the car, and the handsome green limousine sped away.

Donald looked up at the gay, flapping birds. "Painted pigeons! Pooh! When I get so famous that they want to paint things for me—boy! I'll tell them to let the pigeons go, and paint up *El Presidente*."

He strutted off along the promenade.

105

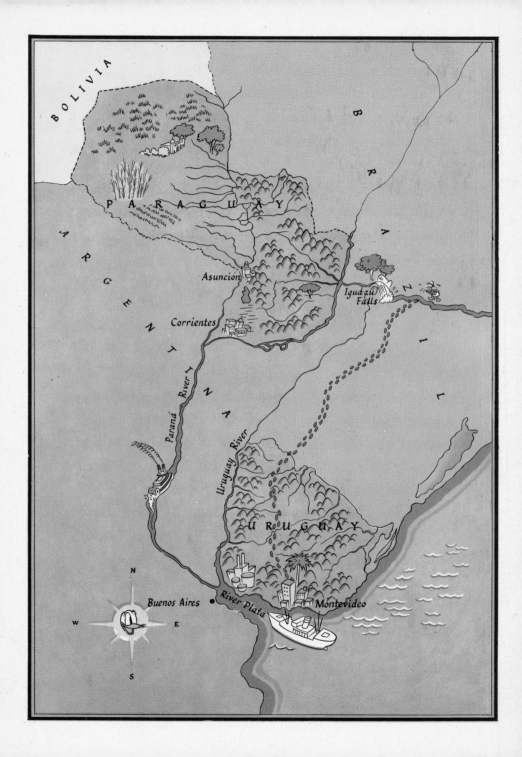

CHAPTER XIII

Troubles in Paraguay and Uruguay

The next afternoon, Donald took a little steamer up the River Plata, for a short visit to Paraguay and Uruguay, the two small Latin-American republics that lie between Argentina and Brazil.

For a while, everything went very well. The ship cruised through the quiet tropics past pleasant little farm villages, old Jesuit missions, and neat, flat plantations of indigo, *maté*, and sugar. Every afternoon Donald sipped *maté* on deck with the agreeable Paraguayan crew, watching the river birds.

But alas! Exactly one week later, battered and tattered, Donald was writing the following letter:

Below Iguazu Falls

My dear nephews:

I am writing this letter with berry juice because there is no ink in this cave. You may wonder why I came here.

It all happened like this. There I was, on the top of these famous South American falls. I said FALLS.

Not one falls like Niagara, but sixty falls, crashing over the jungle cliffs together! Crashbang! There I was up on top in a rowboat, with a guide, snapping snapshots with my Brownie camera. Then, all of a sudden, my guide shouted something in Spanish.

What I thought he said was, "The water isn't really as dangerous as it looks. Why don't you step out, sir, and wade?"

I did. By the time the water had swept me over the falls and forty miles down the rapids, I understood that I don't understand Spanish at all.

I shall leave this letter on a twig, hoping that it will be seen and picked up by some passing river boat. Now I shall beat my way out of here across the swamps and brush. Nothing will stop me till I reach civilization, and hire the best Spanish tutor in all of South America.

Good-by (I am running out of berry juice),

Your Uncle Donald

Several weeks later, scratched, mosquito-bitten, ragged, and weary, Donald limped into Montevideo, the capital of Uruguay. He went straight to a hotel, and settled himself in a room with a balcony.

He picked up the telephone beside the bed. "I

wish to advertise for something in the newspaper—
in all the newspapers," he said.

"Certainly, *señor*," answered the operator. "You've
just time to catch tomorrow morning's editions."

"It goes like this," said Donald. "Help wanted.
Bright pupil—that's me—"

"Yes," said the operator.

"Bright pupil," continued Donald, "obliging,
prompt, obedient, neat, tidy, loyal, brave—"

"Each word costs one *peso*. Haven't you said
enough, *señor?*" interrupted the operator, timidly.

"Not nearly enough! Where was I?"

"'Loyal, brave,'" answered the operator.

"Courageous, fearless, bold, heroic—"

"Is that all, *señor?*"

"Certainly not! But that will do for now. I'm a
very busy person. Just add 'wants Spanish tutor.'"

Before Donald was out of bed the next morning,
there came a knock at the door. Not just one knock
—two, three, four, five—a dozen—two dozen—three
dozen knocks.

Donald jumped up and rushed to the door in
his pajamas. He flung it wide open. A crowd! Not
one tutor but fifty came rushing, galloping into
the room, all jabbering in Spanish at once.

109

"Wonderful!" cried Donald. "Come in, all of you. With fifty tutors, I'll learn fifty times as fast! Begin! Teach me! There's no time to lose. You can start right now, while I'm taking my bath!"

Donald ran into the bathroom; the tutors pressed right on behind. "Cold water!" cried Donald, splashing his face. "How do you say it?"

"*Agua fria!*"

"Hot water. Donald takes shower," sang out Donald, leaping behind the shower curtain and turning on the faucets full blast.

"*Agua caliente. Donaldo toma un bano,*" they

shouted, drowning out the roar of the water. All fifty pushed and shoved to crowd into the bathroom. They pointed at the lights, the ceiling, the walls, the faucets, calling out the names in Spanish.

Donald, dripping, peeked around the corner of the shower curtain and learned each name as they named it. He learned bath towel, bath mat, steam, and ouch! He learned to say a whole Spanish sentence: "I like to squeeze the slippery, green hotel soap."

Then they all went down to the patio to have breakfast under the palm trees. Donald ordered fifty different breakfasts for his fifty tutors, fifty different fruits and fifty cereals. "And," he said to the waiter, "I want fifty different kinds of buttered toast." No one was allowed to eat anything until Donald had seen it and written its name down on the white tablecloth.

All morning they drove through the handsome wide boulevards, the parks, and the famous rose gardens, in a long procession of cars. Six tutors rode with Donald and talked to him; when they lost their voices, they jumped out and six other tutors jumped in. They took him to the Plaza Independencia, where he learned the names of all

112

the government buildings. They drove him to the beaches, the railroad station, and the zoo.

Day after day in the capital city of Uruguay, Donald learned hundreds and thousands of words.

Night after night, while Donald lay in his bed in deep exhausted sleep, his tutors kept the lessons going. All night long they read to him in Spanish.

The last night of his stay in the city, Donald paid the tutors off, and each one gave him a diploma.

Donald had never felt so happy. "I've conquered Spanish faster than any man before me!" he said to himself, stuffing the fifty diplomas down in his golf bag and packing everything to go to Brazil.

He stepped out onto his balcony in his bathrobe. What a night! The tall palm trees in the spacious plazas were waving gently; the moon was shimmering on the bay. Donald felt marvelous.

"At last I speak Spanish! I think Spanish! I walk and I breathe in Spanish! From now on, if I wheeze or if I sneeze, if I cough or if I hiccough, let it be in Spanish!"

He went inside and jumped into bed. "If I dream, I shall dream in Spanish." He crawled in under the luxurious satin quilt. "And if I snore, let me snore in Spanish, too."

CHAPTER XIV

Snakes and Coffee in Brazil

"Nobody in all Brazil can speak the language better than I do," said Donald proudly to himself as he strutted into a restaurant in the busy, modern Brazilian city of São Paulo.

A waiter bowed him to a table and handed him an enormous crimson menu, printed in gold.

Donald refused it. He did not need a menu. He had the name of every food in the Spanish language right there on the tip of his tongue. "Let's see—I'll start with some oysters and a soup." He turned to the waiter. "*Algunas ostiones y una sopa.*"

The waiter scratched his head, and opened the menu in front of Donald.

Donald slammed it shut. "I know what I want. Bring me," he repeated, "*algunas ostiones y una sopa.*"

The waiter looked very much confused. "*Señor,* would you be so kind as to order in English?"

"*English!*" cried Donald in horror.

"*Si, señor.* For North Americans we have Eng-

115

lish menu—see?" He opened the menu again and politely placed it in front of Donald.

Donald sprang to his feet and flung his napkin on the floor. "I don't want to speak English! I want to speak your language!"

"Ah! I see!" The head waiter beamed. "You want to speak our language—Portuguese!"

"Portuguese!" Donald gasped. Three weeks of preparation, fifty tutors wasted! The language of Brazil wasn't Spanish at all! The language of Brazil was Portuguese! This was the last straw!

Donald tore the crimson menu into a hundred small pieces and threw it on the floor. Then he rushed pell-mell out through the big doors that led to the garden terrace.

He stamped and shouted; he picked up handfuls of the gravel walk and hurled them into the goldfish pond; he plunged through the thick hibiscus hedge and made for the wide open country where he would not have to talk to anyone, in any language.

A few hours later Donald found himself sitting on a fence, outside a small enclosure of trees that looked like a park. A gardener was digging around in the earth close by.

"Hey!" called Donald, pointing to the enclosure. "What's in there?"

The gardener looked up, very surprised. "*Instituto Serumtherapico.*"

"*Instituto* what?" Donald jumped down and pushed his way through the thick trees. What was it? A zoo?

He hurried toward a long, flat enclosure, surrounded by a concrete wall and a shallow moat. Inside, just a few feet apart in the grass, stood dozens of little stone igloos. Snakes of all sorts and sizes were wriggling in and out of the igloo doorways. Some were sunning themselves on the roofs; others were sleeping in tangled piles of yellow, brown, and black-and-white spots.

In front of one of these snake huts an attendant in a white coat and high boots was talking in English to some tourists standing in a group outside the rail: "We have about one hundred and eighty different species of snakes in here, mostly from the Amazon jungles. Through the work of this Institute, death from snake-bite has been reduced from 90 to 3 per cent."

Then he explained how they got the venom from the snakes and made it into serum. He tapped one of the igloos with his pole. A snake's head darted out. He grabbed it from behind, by the neck. Then in front of the snake's face he thrust a glass that had a sheet of rubber stretched tightly across the top,

118

like a drum. "This is a rattler," he said, "just watch—"

The snake, angry at being picked up by the neck, struck through the rubber with his fangs, leaving two little amber drops of his venomous liquid there in the glass.

"When this venom," the attendant went on, "is injected into an animal, such as a horse, it does not kill him because the animal is strong enough to build up an anti-venom to fight the poison. From this powerful anti-venom we make the precious serums that have saved thousands of human lives all over the world."

At the close of the attendant's speech, Donald was just about to wander off with the other tourists, when somebody called out in English, from behind him, "How do you do?"

Donald wheeled about. A strange-looking little person came dancing toward him over the grass. He had green pants, a red necktie, and a yellow hat. But the strangest thing of all was the way he was pretending to play music on his beautiful purple umbrella. It was all rolled up tight, and he held it like a flute.

Donald gaped. The person went on bouncing

around in a sort of two-step, blowing into imaginary flute holes on the sides of the umbrella.

"Who are you?" asked Donald, unable to stifle his curiosity any longer.

The person bowed, pulled out a calling card from his pocket, and handed it to Donald:

José C. Carioca

Brasil

"Hmmmm," said Donald. "Then I suppose your language is Portuguese."

"Yes," nodded Jo. "But I also speak a little Spanish, a little English, and many other languages, too. By the way, have you any money?"

"Certainly, lots of money."

"In that case," said Jo, smiling and bowing, "we'll get along just fine. I'd like to have the honor of escorting you to the Carnival in Rio."

Jo seemed to have everything already arranged. He led Donald out to a waiting car. "Step in," said Jo. "I've hired this for you to make the fifty-mile trip to Santos on the coast. Then we'll go on to Rio by boat."

The road to Santos, the great coffee port of Brazil and of the whole world, wound down through fantastically beautiful cliffs and steep gorges. White, foamy mountain torrents cascaded through the midst of purple-green woods.

Then Donald began to smell coffee, stronger and stronger, as they approached the great plantations. Soon he could see nothing in any direction but miles and miles of luxurious coffee trees.

Jo drew in a deep breath of the fragrant aroma. "My country supplies two thirds of all the world's coffee, and the best of it grows right here near São Paulo," he said proudly. "Some of these trees are a hundred years old."

As the car twisted around a curve, it brushed against some tree branches laden with dark red berries, hanging over the road. Donald reached out and plucked off a cluster. "Hmmm," he said, examining them closely. "Who says they're coffee? They look more like cherries to me."

Jo leaned over and took an especially deep red ripe berry out of Donald's hand. He split open the hull and showed Donald the inside. There, in the center, lying face to face, were the two halves of a green coffee bean.

The air grew damp and muggy as they zigzagged on down through the hills toward the sea. Soon Donald could see long rows of freighters tied up three abreast at wharves along the water front. Little freight elevators were creeping down from the tops of the dock warehouses, dumping hundreds of sacks of coffee right into the holds of the waiting ships. In spite of the sleepy, tropical heat, the piers all seethed in hubbub. Dark-skinned stevedores, stripped to the waist, shouted and scurried, unloading coffee from freight cars, coffee from trucks, coffee from wagons. From all the vast plantations near and far, coffee beans were pouring into Santos, ready to be shipped abroad.

They turned into a narrow, crooked little street, crowded with men in white suits, shouting at each other, gesticulating, perspiring, and writing down things in notebooks.

"What's the matter with them all?" asked Donald.

"Nothing. They're coffee brokers, buying and selling coffee and arranging its price. They're deciding what everybody, everywhere in the world, from Turkey to Timbuctoo, will have to pay for his cup of coffee. Come now, here's our boat for Rio."

At a pier just ahead, two ships were tied up: one, a shabby brown freighter; the other, a beautiful, spotless white yacht. The polished brass trimmings of the yacht gleamed in the sunlight, and colored streamers fluttered from its masts.

"Wheeee!" said Donald, rushing out of the car

ahead of Jo, and making for the yacht's gangway. "What a setup!"

"Not this boat," said Jo, grabbing him by the coattails. "That boat—there!" He pointed to the gangway that went up to the shabby freighter.

"But I want to go on the yacht!" cried Donald.

"Alas," sighed Jo, "the yacht is only for the most important visitors. It's waiting here for *El Presidente de la Comisión—*"

"That man! He's got my place again!"

Jo pulled Donald up the rickety gangway of the freighter. As they stepped aboard, the deck officer motioned them back to second class. It was a cattle ship, and all the first-class accommodation was reserved for horses and cows.

CHAPTER XV

Carnival in Rio

"Shhhhh! Calm yourself," said Jo. "You'll wake up the horses."

The little freighter was nosing its way in and out among the fantastic islands of the bay of Rio de Janeiro. In the early dawn light, it seemed to Donald that islands were popping right up out of the water like Jacks-in-the-box.

125

"I can't describe it!" he wailed. "I can't! It's too beautiful! Look at it, Jo!" Donald was pacing around in dizzy circles on the forward deck, tearing up his unwritten diary and throwing the tiny white pieces up into the air.

"I am looking at it," said Jo. "Why describe it? Nobody's ever been able to describe Rio."

The shore line of the coast zigzagged around curving beaches of silvery sand. The mountains behind the city cut into the clouds with sharp cones and spires that kept changing color from purple to blue and pink in the mysterious morning light. Soon they were flecked with patches of gold and vermilion. The sun was getting more brilliant every minute; it danced on the wires of the cable car that swung up to Sugar Loaf pinnacle and along the red roofs of the houses on the green jungle slopes.

"Come," said Jo, jumping up with a start. "We're almost at the wharf." He began doing his little bouncing two-step toward the gangway.

"What do you call that?" said Donald.

"Samba," said Jo. "It's the Carnival step. You'll learn. Just wait till tonight."

When Donald walked ashore in Rio, he thought he was walking in a dream. The royal palms rose

up so high that he had to lean way over backwards
to see the tops. The sidewalks were paved with
mosaics in dizzy black-and-white zebra stripes.
There were parks with fountains, bright flowers
everywhere, and cool shade trees along the streets.
There were shop windows sparkling with Brazilian
diamonds, aquamarines, sapphires, and topazes.

Jo took him from café to café where men in
white suits were having coffee with pretty women.
They drank it black from little cups, pouring in

sugar from big pitchers as though it were cream.

Everyone seemed very excited. All the while they drank their coffee, they tapped with their feet on the white-tiled floor. Everyone was doing the samba. Carnival was in the air.

Donald and Jo spent the rest of the day in their hotel room, making a Carnival costume. Out of a fur rug they made a llama, with a long, shaggy neck and a tail of braided wool.

"You be the back, and I'll be the front legs," said Jo. "You don't know where to go and I do."

Gay evening music floated in through the window just as the llama suit was ready. Drums! Flutes! Trombones! Donald raced across the room and looked out. False faces! Red wigs! Fancy costumes! Clowns! A whole parade of funny kings and queens!

Donald and Jo hustled into their llama suit.

Right down the main stairway into the lobby galloped the shaggy beast. Then his front legs started to samba and his back legs danced the samba, too. Ladies in long skirts swished up to admire. Out to the street they went, all dancing together. They threw confetti; they squirted perfume at each other from little toy guns.

Hour after hour they danced in and out of all

the cafés of Rio. Sometimes ladies gave the llama candy. Jo got it all because he was the head.

Then, suddenly, a peculiar thing happened. As Donald danced along, crouched low in the back part of the llama suit, he saw a newspaper lying on the white-tiled floor. A name in the middle of the Portuguese headline made him gasp. WHELPLEY! He snatched the newspaper off the floor, but he could not read it because it was in Portuguese. He had to show it to Jo.

The llama's hind legs trotted up beside the the front legs. Donald reached out an arm and held up the paper before the animal's eyes. The Carnival merrymakers choked with laughter as the fore part of the llama began reading a newspaper out loud to the hind part.

"Mr. D. Appley Whelpley," translated Jo, "feared lost in Amazon jungle. Whelpley last seen leaving rubber plantation near Manáos."

"Mr. Whelpley lost!" cried Donald. "Then there is something about South America that Mr. Whelpley doesn't know. Oh, boy, will I show him!"

Donald sprang out of the back part of the llama suit, and ripped the front part off Jo. For them, the Carnival was over; the Whelpley hunt was on.

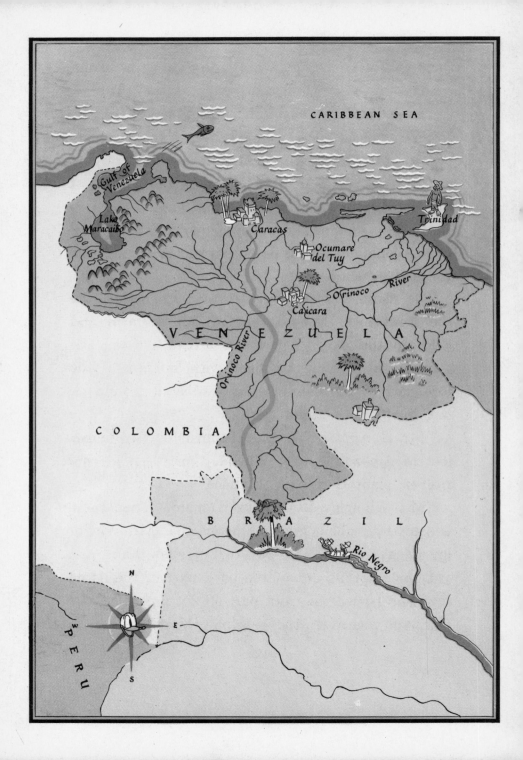

CHAPTER XVI

Through the Amazon Jungles to Venezuela

A week later Donald and Jo, in a plane specially chartered by Donald and piloted by Jo, arrived at Manáos, far, far up in the Amazon country. There they soon found their first clue—the launch in which Mr. Whelpley had left his plantation.

The boat was stuck on a mud flat, facing north, in the center of the river. Mr. Whelpley's suitcase, his overcoat, and a box of enormous green gumdrops were piled together in the bow.

After talking it over, they bought a camping outfit, two ladders, mosquito netting, eleven chocolate bars, and a stewpot. Then they headed north, too, by canoe.

They paddled upstream, following the Rio Negro, which branched out here from the main course of the Amazon. The water was black and murky, blacker than the dark forests which stretched in all directions as far as they could see.

Paddling was tiring work, and they were glad

to stop to make camp. Donald climbed out of the canoe into the wildest country he had ever seen.

In the forest the earth smelled moist and hot. It steamed up around him like hot perfume. Squash! His feet sank down in a wet, spongy carpet of flowers. There were fuchsias, crimson and white begonias, pink and green orchids on sprays three and four feet long. He trampled on orchids everywhere.

Gradually Donald's eyes became accustomed to the darkness. The trees that had all looked alike from the boat actually were all very different. Palms, myrtles, laurels, acacias, rubber trees, hundreds of trees of all shapes and sizes were crowding each other, fighting for space in which to grow.

Donald picked some ripe juicy figs. Papayas, chirimoyas, mangoes, and Brazil nuts just waiting to be eaten were lying on the ground among the flowers.

Up on the highest level, the roof of the forest flamed with brilliant blossoms. Leaves rustled and fluttered as gorgeous birds flew in and out and monkeys darted from branch to branch. All sorts of strange creatures were living up there in the tangle of branches and vines.

"Hey!" It was Jo. "Come and see what I've got."

Donald hurried back to the river's edge.

Jo had put up the tent on the sand bank, had made a fire, and was roasting something on a spit. Something else was stewing in the stewpot. Jo had made himself a comfortable mattress of river grass, and was lying on it, munching one of Mr. Whelpley's enormous green gumdrops.

"Roast turtle," said Jo proudly, "and steamed water lettuce."

Night came on very suddenly. The air was bright and clear. Donald wrapped himself up in his mosquito netting and lay on the floor of the tent. Beside him on the floor, Jo lay lounging, contented, balancing still another of Mr. Whelpley's green gumdrops on the tip of his black umbrella.

A woodpecker, pecking at the tentpole, woke them up at dawn. Donald bustled out to load the canoe. The river banks were actually crowded with all sorts of magnificently colored water birds: herons, spoonbills, scarlet ibises, and huge marabou storks.

Donald and Jo stowed everything away neatly in the broad bottom of the canoe—the two ladders they balanced across the boat again.

Paddling upstream was no easy task, but Donald

kept them going steadily forward against the muddy current, while the river twisted and curved.

Jo lay luxuriously in the bow, scanning the brush and treetops with the binoculars.

"I think I see an eagle," said Jo, straining to examine a speck on the very top of a solitary giant palm tree, half a mile ahead. "No, it isn't an eagle. Maybe it's a condor!" Jo suddenly stood up, almost upsetting the boat. "I think it's a man!"

"Man!" Donald leapt across the ladders and scrambled up to the bow. He grabbed the binoculars. "Jiminy! It's Mr. Whelpley!"

Donald paddled furiously ahead, and even Jo paddled too. They could hardly believe what they saw. Mr. Whelpley was sprawled limply over the treetop, like an oversized, droopy rag doll.

They pulled up to the bank, and while Jo dragged along the ropes and the ladders, Donald ran ahead.

"Here I am!" cried Donald as he raced up under the tree. "You're rescued, Mr. Whelpley!"

Slowly Mr. Whelpley opened his eyes and looked down, but he did not answer. He just smiled.

Quickly they bound the ladders together and stood them against the tree, but the ladders did not quite reach to the top.

"We'll use mountain-climbing tricks," said Donald, "and rope ourselves together."

The rescue party scrambled up the ladders. Higher and higher they climbed. At the top of

the second ladder, Donald made a lasso of rope and tied it around his waist. He flung the lasso over the tree's topmost tuft and yanked it tight. Then, hand over hand, he pulled himself up. "Put your arms around my neck, Mr. Whelpley," he shouted. "I'll carry you down on my back."

Obediently, but dumbly, Mr. Whelpley obeyed.

Then, carefully, Donald, with Jo just below him, climbed down the ladder again, and dropped with his burden safely onto the ground.

"Now," said Donald, as Mr. Whelpley got up and stretched, "would you mind telling me how you happened to get up there?"

Mr. Whelpley looked very blank. He looked up at the tree and looked blanker still. He scratched his head. "You know, I just don't remember."

"Lost his memory," said Jo calmly. "It happens to lots of people that get lost in the jungle. They have to start all over again and learn everything right from scratch."

"Everything?" asked Donald. "You mean he doesn't know anything at all about South America?"

"Nothing," said Jo. "Not one blessed thing."

"Boy! Oh, boy!" cried Donald. "Will I enjoy teaching him!"

He turned to Mr. Whelpley. "You see, sir, what I don't know about South America just isn't worth knowing at all!"

Day after day and week after week, as they made their way northward, Donald, the teacher, taught Mr. Whelpley, the pupil. In canoes, in ox-carts, and on mule-back, Donald retaught Mr. Whelpley the important facts about South America.

By the time they finally reached Caracas, the capital of Venezuela, Mr. Whelpley was a fairly well-educated man. And Donald was famous. News of his daring rescue of Mr. Whelpley from the jungle treetop had been carried ahead to every village by the Indians.

On a special platform erected in the Plaza Bolivar, the Mayor officially welcomed them to Caracas. Flags flew from the public buildings; brass bands played all the national anthems; confetti filled the air. The children in the city schools were excused from their classes to take part in the hero's reception. As Donald and his party marched into the Plaza, the people cheered wildly and flung their hats at the broiling sun.

Every distinguished official made a long speech

137

in Spanish; Donald made the longest speech of all, and spoke in Spanish too.

Donald's triumphant tour was over. It was time to say *adiós* to all his Latin-American friends. It was time to take the plane back home.

"Everything has been arranged, *Señor* Donald," said the Mayor, "for your comfort on the plane."

"Everything?" asked Donald. "Are you sure I have a seat that no one can take—not even *El Presidente de la Comisión de la—*"

"My dear young fellow!" laughed the Mayor heartily, slapping Donald on the back. "This time *El Presidente* is just out of luck. You have his priority!"

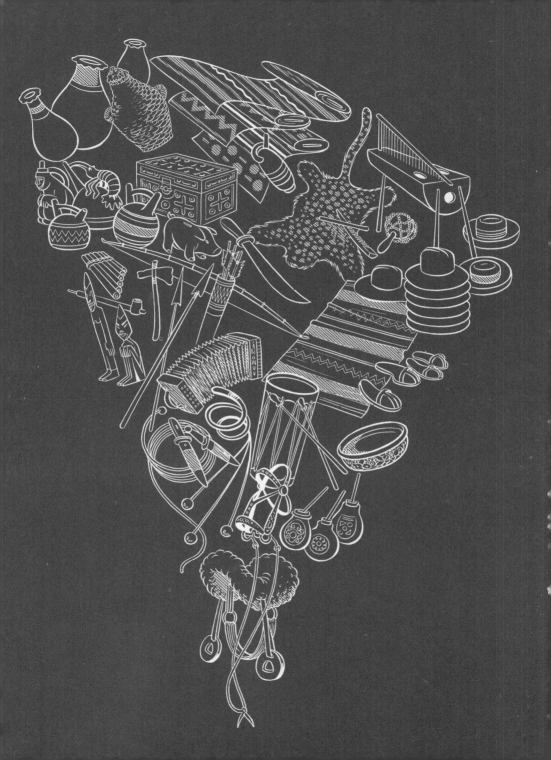